Erotic Street Blues

First Edition

Christopher Trevor

Erotic Street Blues

First Edition

Published by The Nazca Plains Corporation
Las Vegas, Nevada
2007

ISBN: 978-1-887895-97-2

Published by

The Nazca Plains Corporation ®
4640 Paradise Rd, Suite 141
Las Vegas NV 89109-8000

PUBLISHER'S NOTE
Erotic Street Blues is a work of fiction created wholly by
Christopher Trevor's imagination. All characters are fictional and
any resemblance to any persons living or deceased is purely
by accident. No portion of this book reflects any real person or
events.

Cover, Greasetank
Art Director, Blake Stephens

Erotic Street Blues

Christopher Trevor

Contents

Captured Cop

The two burly and overly rugged men were outside in the warm sun, thoroughly enjoying themselves in the back of the big house that the bigger of the two men owned. The house was mansion-like, huge, situated by itself and surrounded by nothing but deep and dense woods. It was the only house on the long road that we had driven on for miles upon miles after they had captured me. Fucking fucks, but they had managed to capture me after I had pulled them over for driving way above the speed limit. Fucking totally fucks, nothing is worse for a cop than having the drop on him, worse if the perpetrator that gets the drop on you decides to kidnap your handsome ass. In my case two perpetrators had captured me, although when I had given chase to the speeding car I thought that there was only one guy in there, the driver obviously. That had been the mistake that got me captured, more on that soon. I have a long and miserable story to tell and I want all cops to hear it so that they don't make the same mistake I did. The bigger of the two guys was stretched out on a lounge chair in the warm sun as the other guy knelt submissively next to him, stroking his big cock for him. The two exceedingly muscular men were wearing nothing but jeans and construction boots, their huge beefy cocks and juicy balls sticking out of the fly openings of their jeans. Their rock-hard muscular bodies' glistened in the sun, sweaty and smelling real raunchy and manly. The bigger guy squeezed and twisted the fuck out of his erect man-sized nipples as his buddy stroked his pre cum slicked cock faster for him, bringing him closer to the impending gusher.

"Oh yeah, stroke my meat man, play with my damned skin

flute," the bigger of the two men grunted, sounding breathless, his massive upper body arching itself slightly up off the lounge chair. "I'm getting close buddy, real fucking close now."

The guy kneeling submissively next to the lounge chair leaned down and slurped his buddies pulsing meat stick deep into his craw and began stroking himself as he sucked his foul mouthed crony like crazy.

"Ohhhhhhhhhhhrrrrr yeah, fuck yeah, fucking A, that's it man, *that is the fucking ticket,*" the bigger man said throatily, squeezing and twisting the bejesus out of his own nips as he was now being sucked toward a gusher. "Suck my big meat man, suck the fuck outa me real good bud..."

He lay back on the lounge chair, his big booted feet on the ground at the sides of the chair. His buddy slobbered messily over his big cock and quickly sucked it all back up, heartily sucking his bud's cock at the same time, stroking himself as well. It was a real raunchy and sexy free for all out there on that lounge chair. The guy kneeling on the ground was doing all the work, but obviously enjoying himself all the while. With the big guy's cock in his mouth he stroked himself with two hands; his cock was that big, his head bobbing up and down as he worked his magic...

As for me, the poor cop telling this tirade, I was at the moment nearby the two men, struggling fruitlessly. Fuck, they had me locked in a wooden tool shed, my wrists cinched in my own damned handcuffs behind me and around a wooden post. How awful is that? How awful is it for a cop to be snagged in his own handcuffs? My feet were securely tied to the bottom of the post with mounds of tightly wound white cotton rope around my ankles and just about up to my calves. I was clad in just my police issued lace-up black clonky shoes, my knee length black nylon dress socks (what the executive's of the world nowadays refer to as OTC socks, OTC meaning over the calf) and my utility belt hung loosely around my waist, mocking the fucking fuck out of me. My utility belt was minus my gun, my radio and my baton. My gun had been the first thing the two men had confiscated upon capturing me, obviously. My radio, my only contact to headquarters dispatch was with the two men, so that they could keep an ear out for any rescue attempts that my cop brothers might be making on my behalf, their captured buddy. By the time headquarters dispatch had realized that I was in trouble I was long gone, kidnapped by the two men I had planned on giving a speeding ticket to. Without my radio on my person there was no way for my police brothers to contact me. My semi (fear) hard cock was twitching under my utility belt, dribbling beads of piss and slimy pre cum, humiliating! My succulent hairy balls hung below my cock and utility belt like a damned chandelier. My uniform was thrown on a dusty chair at the other end of the tool shed. That was where they'd made me put it after forcing me (at gunpoint) to strip when they'd brought me to this godforsaken destination. How could this have befallen me I thought miserably as I struggled to what I knew would be no avail in my damned handcuffs. I had small hopes of perhaps knocking down the post I was trussed up to, getting my handcuffed wrists under my legs and end up bringing them in front of me. All of that before the two men outside the woodshed heard what the fuck was happening and snagged me again, *right!*

The post, unfortunately was embedded in the concrete floor of the shed and the top of it was supported by a ceiling beam, no chance whatsofuckingever of carrying out my little escape plan. And even if I did manage to get my cuffed wrists in front of me I didn't have my damned handcuff key. The two men had confiscated that as well, after my little escape stint back in the car, more on that later as well. My nametag and my badge I hate to have to admit to you where they'd pinned them for the time being, the time they were making me wait till they got around to round one of working me over. My nametag was pinned to my left nipple, piercing it and my badge was pierced to my other nipple. God almighty, the pain when they had totally skewered my poor nipples I cannot even begin to tell you. And not before they had each slurped and sucked my big cop tits up to erect and totally rigid. Fuck, never had any damned faggots eating my man sized cop tits before let me just state for the record. And now, I still had no clue whatsofuckingever of what they planned to do with me, although I did have some pretty nasty and unthinkable ideas. I mean, what else would two sadistic faggots do to a cop once they'd captured him? My baton was laid across my uniform, also mocking me like my utility belt minus my gun and radio. I wondered dishearteningly if they planned to use it on me in different ways than they'd used it on me already. God, whacked and beaten with my own baton and cinched in my own handcuffs, what a fucked up turn of events that day! Leaning against the post in the wooden tool shed, my smooth muscular and bruised barrel-like muscular chest and pecs jutting out all robust and sweaty I suddenly heard the sounds of the huge lug swearing in ecstasy as he shot his big load of creamy man's spunk.

"Ohhhhhhhhrrrrr yeah bud, that's it, fucking "A", again man, aaaaarrrrrrrhhhh yeah," the big dude grunted breathlessly, squeezing and twisting his nipples as his buddy stroked his mess from him. "OHHHHHHRRR yeah, fucking stud you are man!! Lookit this shit got me cumming like goddamned gangbusters here!!"

His massively muscled body was arched up on the lounge chair and listening to him from inside my woodshed prison I struggled even more to somehow get free, yet at the same time knowing it was no use. My handcuffs made jangling sounds as I pounded my cinched wrists against the back of the post. The over-sized muscles in my upper arms flexed involuntarily and my biceps bulged real big with my fruitless efforts. Fuck, now that the big lug had shot his load it would be his buddies turn next. Then they would be coming in the shed to have some sinister and twisted fun with me, Police Officer Scott Reed, upstate New York City police officer to be exact. As I stood there in just my shoes, my socks and my utility belt with my semi hardness-pointing straight out I thought back to how I had come to be in this most miserable of all predicaments, a predicament that no cop should ever find themselves in. As I thought about my dilemma, I heard the sounds of slurping as the big guy gobbled his buddies' meat stick into his mouth... My semi hardness between my legs tingled in a mixture of fear and frustration of some kind... Beads of piss and droplets of pre cum oozed from my wide sexy cock slit...

"Ohhhhhhhh yeah, suck my muscle pipe now man, fuck yeah, we'll have a real sexy warm-up out here and then we'll get to our handsome cop," the second guy grunted.

He now lay on the lounge chair squeezing and twisting his fat nipples while his big buddy suckled the fuck out of his cock.

As I said, my name is Scott Reed, Officer Scott Reed. I've been a New York City police officer now for the last three years, and damned proud of it too if I may say so myself. I'm twenty-four years old. I have thin black hair, cut real short, practically military style. The only other hair on my body is in my armpits and on my big luscious and succulent balls. I have intense dark eyes and at five feet nine inches tall, my body is rock hard and well toned from the daily workouts I put myself through at the gym every night after I get off duty. Being that I live in Yonkers I'm stationed in the upstate area of New York City. I was on a daily and routine patrolling the day of my capture. It was a muggy July afternoon and I thanked God that my police cruiser was air-conditioned. Dressed in my navy blue police uniform I was cruising along just under the speed limit on a lonely deserted road in the woodsy area of upstate when seemingly out of nowhere a car sped past me, blowing exhaust fumes and smoke all over the road as it went, nearly side-swiping me by mere inches...

"HOLY FUCKING SHIT!!!" I roared and clenched my teeth in anger, realizing that the car had come up onto the road from the last entrance I had just passed on the lonely highway.

The roar of the car as it sped past me was deafening for a moment, startling the fucking fucks out of me, but being the good clear headed cop that I am I reacted instantly. I pushed the pedal nearly to the floor, turned on the overhead lights and siren, gripped the steering wheel with one hand and gave chase.

"FUCKING law breaker!!" I ranted angrily, reaching down with my other hand for my dispatch hand-held radio receiver. "Fucker nearly ran me off the road! Man, I am going to make sure this guy spends the next few weeks behind bars!!"

I ranted and seethed all types of obscenities as I gained on the car before speaking into my hand-held radio transmitter.

"This is Reed, I am presently in pursuit of a speeding car on interstate two forty five," I said. "Come back."

"We roger that Reed," the female voice at dispatch replied. "What is the make and license plate of the car you are in pursuit of?"

"Looks to be a dark blue Monte Carlo," I replied. "Can't say for sure, negative on the license plate at this time. The driver is speeding recklessly and so fast that the smoke from his exhaust and the road dust he's kicking up is blocking my view of the plate."

"How many suspects are in the car Reed?" the disembodied dispatch voice asked.

"Just the driver," I replied through clenched teeth as I sped faster behind the car.

I put the radio down and coughing on the driver's exhaust smoke I signaled for him to pull over, the muscles in my arm burning with anger as I held it out my now rolled down car window. After a few more moments of chase the guy in the car finally slowed down. I did the same, killing the siren and flashing lights on the roof of my cruiser. I fleetingly thought how it seemed like he wanted to be caught, the way he had sped past a cop and all, but sadly, I only thought that fleetingly. When he came to a full stop I grabbed the microphone in my car and spoke angrily into it.

"Stay in the car!!" I spat irately. "I repeat, stay in the car!! Do not move and keep your hands on the steering wheel!!" After issuing my orders I pulled my cruiser up a few feet from his car and slowly stepped out of it. With the heat of the sun beating down on my head, I put on my uniform hat. I wasn't out of the car more than three seconds or so and I was sweating in my short-sleeved uniform shirt, the muscles in my arms bulging with anger in the sleeves. My police issued highly shined black shoes crunched on the pavement of the highway as I sidled up to the car, my hand near my holster. I noticed, but made no mention of

it that the back trunk of the car was slightly open. I simply figured that that would add to this guy's misery when I arrested him
and gave him the ticket for speeding. Had I been sharp enough
to check that slightly opened trunk first before approaching the
driver it might have saved me a lot of anguish. It might have pre-
vented the two men from making off with me.

"Good afternoon Officer..." the guy in the car said to me
as he sat there with his big meaty looking hands on the steering
wheel, the window rolled down on the driver's side, him glancing
up at my nametag.

"Reed, Officer Reed, *wow,* just like in that old cop TV
series back in the early seventies, Officer Reed, handsomest cop
in TV land."

"Sir, may I please see your driver's license?" I asked the
guy, ignoring what he'd just said in reference to my name, but
God alone knew how many times I'd been teased and razzed
about that by my cop brothers and buddies of mine. "And use
your fingers only to reach for your wallet. I want your hands right
where I can see them at all times!!"

"Not to worry Officer Reed, I'm not armed," the guy said,
obeying my orders.

"I didn't ask you that Sir," I said sternly.

He got his wallet out of the back pocket of his jeans, took
out his driver's license and handed it to me. I looked at it and saw
that it was indeed a valid driver's license. The guy's first name
was Otis but the last name had a smudge of some sort over it,
obscuring it.

"Please step slowly out of the car," I said, taking a couple
of steps back to give him ample room.

The door of the car opened with a loud creaking sound,
masking the sound of the trunk of the car being slowly opened
by the other guy who had been hiding in there. The guy named
Otis stepped out of the car and stood before me in all his muscular glory. I could tell from the way his white tee shirt was pressing against his arms and chest that he was built like a brick shit
house, his nips making two points against his shirt, it was that

tight against his chest muscles. He was also wearing worn looking blue jeans and construction worker style mustard colored boots. I guessed his height to be about six feet and he had a dopey but sinister look about him.

"Did I do something wrong Officer Reed?" Otis asked me.

"Driving at nearly eighty miles an hour in a thirty-five mile an hour zone is doing something wrong I would say," I barked at him. "Not coming to a complete stop when you saw an officer of the law pursuing you is doing something wrong I would say. Endangering that officer's life by making him speed as well is doing something wrong I would say! Now, let's find out if you're under the influence."

I took another few steps back, my hands now held out in front of me, ready to catch the guy if he tottered, if he was at all intoxicated. I didn't know that taking my hand away from my holster was not the smartest thing to do at that moment. I also didn't know that with each step back that I took I was walking backward into a shit load of trouble.

"Please walk a few straight steps toward me Sir!" I said commandingly.

"I assure you Officer, I have not been drinking," Otis said to me, flashing a shit-eating grin.

"Just do as you're being told buddy," I replied sternly and watched as the big lug took a couple of straight steps.

Suddenly, from behind me I felt what felt like the muzzle of a gun pressed hard into my lower back.

"Not a move Officer Stupid," I heard a husky sounding voice say from behind me. "And keep *your hands* right where *I* can see them!"

I instantly froze in terror and my eyes opened wide in shock at this sudden turn of the tables.

"Son of a bitch," I muttered through my clenched teeth.

Now I knew why the trunk of the car had been slightly opened. Fuck, the other dude had been crouched down in there the whole time. This was looking more and more like an evil plan to snag a cop.

"Now, slowly, raise your hands, you know the way I'm sure," the voice from behind me said with total confidence, pressing what felt like the muzzle of the gun harder into my lower back.

I gulped hard and reluctantly and sadly moved my hands and arms straight up in the shape of two letters "L."

"Good boy Officer Stupid," the guy behind me said and still pressing what felt like the muzzle of a gun into my lower back confiscated the gun in my holster.

I felt a twang of pain in my heart as my gun was taken from me. Otis was standing in front of me grinning sadistically from ear to ear at my peril.

"Y-you guys are making this real difficult on yourselves," I said through trembling lips as the guy behind me sidled up next to me, my gun in his hand, in his other hand a sawed off broom handle. "Fuck, it wasn't a gun you had pressed into my back, man, *you weren't even armed!!*"

"No, but I sure as shit am now," the guy with my gun in hand said meanly. "And besides, I did you a favor Officer Stupid. I didn't bash you over your handsome head with that broom handle!"

Grinning as sadistically as Otis the handsome muscular hunk tossed the sawed off broom handle under my police cruiser. I gulped again and sick at heart now realized how I had been had. In total anguish I slowly curled my hands into loose fists, getting ready to make my move.

"Looks like a good catch as usual Otis," the bigger of the two guys said. "Never thought that we would land such a handsome officer of the law, but as the saying goes, what the fuck?"

He was dressed just as Otis was, in worn jeans a tight tee shirt and mustard colored construction boots.

"L-look man, give me my goddamned gun, you're making a big mistake here," I said to the big lug as he stepped back behind me, my gun held in his hand pointing at my back. "You boys won't get away with this shit! Harassing a police officer is against the law!!"

I curled my raised hands into tight fists, keeping that look of terror on my face, my chest jutted out. At my last remark the two men started laughing, telling me how they were going to do a lot more than just harass me.

"I told you he would pursue me if I sped past him Cleeve," Otis said to his bug buddy. "I've seen this handsome piece of cop ass patrolling this area for the last few days now."

Fuck, *they had been stalking me???* Now I knew for sure that this was a plan to snag a cop.

"I knew he would make a good mark for us," Otis went on, reaching for the baton on my utility belt.

Fuck, fucking fuck, *they were* planning on kidnapping my handsome ass! I seethed inwardly in a mixture of terror and anger, no fucking way I was going to allow this to happen, not without a confrontation at least! As Otis helped himself to my baton I pursed my lips tightly together. One of the mugs had my gun and now the other one was taking my baton, fuck, I was being stripped of my arsenal one piece at a time, but *I was ready.* I whirled around as fast as possible and swung a hard clenched fist at Cleeve's face, hell bent on getting my gun back from him. Fucking fucks, I was ready to kill both of these guys if it came down to that! But Cleeve was fast, and from what I witnessed he'd been dutifully trained in armed combat. As I whirled around, as I threw out my fist he took a few quick steps back from me, causing me to miss my intended target.

"HUUUUUFFFF!!!" I grunted angrily as the big lug pivoted out of my way and my tightly clenched fist hit nothing but air.

As my fist missed Cleeve's jaw he raised my gun, pointed it at my face and pulled the trigger. The sound of the gun only clicking, seeing as the safety was on nearly startled me out of my shoes. The sound of the clicking of my gun a second time as Cleeve tormented me seemed to fill the air around us and from behind me Otis whacked the back of my knees with my baton, hard.

"UHHHHNNNFFFFFF!!!" I grunted at the sudden pain,

the lower part of my legs and calves feeling like they had been turned to jelly.

Cleeve took a step toward me, my gun pointed at my gut. I saw that the safety was now off and Cleeve's finger was slowly pulling the trigger back. My hands instantly flew straight back up, palms open this time, real vulnerable feeling as I wobbled unbalanced on my aching jelly-like legs.

"D-don't man, *don't shoot me!!*" I gasped. *"Please man..."*

"Got a wife and kids Copper?" Cleeve asked me mockingly, clicking the hammer back on my gun. "That's the line all you pigs give when you're in a shit-load of trouble!"

From behind me Otis whacked the back of my upper thighs harder than hard with my baton and at that moment Cleeve rammed me a good hard punch to the old gut, totally knocking the wind out of me.

"HOOOFFFFF!!!" I sputtered and doubled over in pain, my uniform hat falling off my head and landing on the ground.

The pain behind my knees and in my upper thighs was immense. I straightened halfway up and turned slowly to face Otis, a scowl of outright hatred etched on my face. But as I turned Otis rapped me hard across the side of my knees with my baton and then I heard a gunshot fill the air.

"HAAAAARRRRRRRRR FUCK!!!" I roared in total sheer terror now, turning and seeing Cleeve holding my gun pointed at me, the scent of gunpowder filling the air.

Despite the pain I was in I snapped quickly to a stance of near attention and raised my hands high...

I stood before the two men gasping for air, my breath coming short, feeling like I would piss in my uniform pants. My knees and thighs were hurting real bad but for the purposes of my life I managed to stay up on my feet. I was sopped in fear sweat and embarrassingly to say my meat stick was fear hard in my uniform pants. My eyes darted wildly back and forth in real terror anger and frustration as the two men seemed to be looking me over lustfully... I was starting to realize why they had been stalking me and why they had ambushed me.

"Officer Reed, come in, Officer Reed, please respond," my police radio suddenly squawked on my utility belt.

"Ha, if headquarters could see you now Officer Stupid," Cleeve said, holding my gun pointed at my chest as Otis next took my radio off my belt.

Fuck, fuck, double and triple fucks, I felt like a knight slowly being stripped of his armor. I grimaced miserably as Otis turned my radio off and held it up.

"We better get moving Cleeve," Otis said. "No doubt this pig alerted his dispatch when he started pursuing me."

"Yeah, the only thing we want his cop buddies finding when they get here is his abandoned cruiser," Cleeve said.

"You guys are going to pay for this shit!!" I seethed; as I turned back facing Cleeve.

"We don't plan on paying for anything Officer Stupid," Cleeve said to me with a leer on his face, the muzzle of my gun pressed against my belly button. "Not when we can get it for free with you."

Again the two men chortled their laughter loud and mockingly. I gulped hard as Cleeve took a few steps back from me, still holding my gun pointed at me as Otis next took my handcuffs off my belt.

"Okay Officer Stupid, you're going to take a ride with us," Cleeve said and then my heart thundered in mortal terror in my chest. "A long ride to be exact..."

I stood rooted to the spot, my mind in a tailspin as Otis did the honors of locking my wrists behind me, in my own damned handcuffs. With my gun in Cleeve's hand still pointed at me I felt it best at that moment to do as the two men wanted...my time would come soon...I hoped...

"Okay Otis, blindfold the pig and lets get on our way," Cleeve said, stepping over to their car and opening the back trunk.

"Y-you're planning on putting me in the trunk of your car?" I stammered in total fear as Otis tied a white cloth over my eyes, effectively blindfolding me.

"Heh, if it was good enough for me while you were pursuing us then it'll be good enough for you Officer Stupid," Cleeve laughed.

Holding me by my upper arm Otis guided me over to their car and the two men hoisted me roughly into the trunk... They curled my legs back to force me to fit and I admit I was shuddering in fear by then. What had just happened to me is every cop's worst nightmare.

"Let's get going," Cleeve said and I heard the trunk slam shut. "I got a feeling his cop buddies are on the way. I can smell pig in the air.

I shuddered more than in fear as they got into the car and sped off, the only evidence that I had been there were my police cruiser, the broom handle under my cruiser that Cleeve had used to trick me with, and my uniform hat on the ground where they had left it...

It was about ten minutes or so into the ride that I started to think somewhat coherently. So far we had been driving straight on the road, which meant that we were still on the interstate where I had begun my pursuit of the speeding car. As I continued to think coherently I also recalled the fact that like any good cop I didn't keep my handcuff key on my utility belt, rather, I kept it in the back pocket of my uniform pants. Smiling behind the blindfold I slowly wriggled my hand into the left-hand side back pocket of my uniform pants...

As I reached for my key I felt the car turning off the interstate, fuck, no way now of knowing where the fuck they were taking me...

I got my fingers around the key and managed to slowly pull it from my pocket, being super careful not to jostle myself in the confines of the trunk. I didn't want the two guys knowing what I was up to until I had the advantage, entirely...

I managed to make my hands and fingers stop trembling long enough to get my handcuff key out of my back pocket. Then, using only my sense of touch I slowly and methodically worked the key into the tiny hole of the cuff on my right wrist. I held my breath and gave the key a turn. I exhaled with a sigh of relief, only wishing that I had my radio on my person so that I could signal my fellow officers. By now they had found my abandoned cruiser on the road. No doubt a search would be out in full force for the missing officer. But until some kind of help arrived I was essentially on my own... I slipped the key back into my pants pocket...

The car came to a halt more than an hour or so later. By then my legs and arms were feeling pretty numb and awfully cramped from having been restricted for so long. I wondered in horror where they had brought me. I also wondered what my chances for escape were without my baton or gun. Fucking fuck, but I had to try.

"Well here we are Cop, home sweet fucking home at last," I heard Cleeve saying as the two men got out of the car, slamming the doors.

I kept my freed hands behind me, not yet wanting the two men knowing that I had slipped out of my handcuffs. The trunk of the car was pulled open and I felt their hands grabbing my upper arms, hoisting me roughly out of the hot trunk. Once I was on my feet I was prepared to make my move.

"Hope you enjoyed the ride Copper," Cleeve said, straightening my necktie as he spoke. "And if you didn't enjoy the ride, well, we don't give a flying fuck!"

His hand was on my tie and I didn't feel my gun pressing into my back... It was time to make my move...

It was now or never...

I quickly reached up, yanked the blindfold down and away from my eyes and landed a good hard punch to Cleeve's jaw, sending him sprawling to the ground.

"HOOOFFFFF!!!!" Cleeve grunted as he hit the ground. *"Fuck, the pig is free Otis, how the fuck???"*

As I had punched Cleeve my back was turned to Otis. As I turned to pummel him next he beat me to the punch. The guy still had my baton in hand and he used it most skillfully. Like at the time of my capture he rapped me good and fucking hard behind the backs of my knees. Actually, this time he rapped me about a hundred times harder than he had at the time of my capture.

"HARRRRRR!!!" I roared in the blinding pain and fell to the ground on my knees.

As I tried to quickly stand up Otis rapped me again, good and fucking hard this time across my chest with my baton.

"UUUUUHHHNNNFFFFF!!!!" I grunted and found myself sprawled on my stomach this time, flat on the ground.

I did not even recall turning and landing on my front side after Otis had so meanly rapped my pecs.

"OHHHHHHHRRRR GAWD," I groaned miserably, pressing my palms flat against the ground.

"How the fuck did he get himself free???" Otis asked Cleeve angrily. "Those handcuffs were locked tight around his goddamned wrists! I made sure of it."

Squatting over me, my gun in his hand pointed at my back Cleeve reached into the back pocket of my uniform pants… Like a child who's just won an award Cleeve held up my handcuff key.

"This is how he got free," Cleeve said calmly, yet the awful trace of sadism in his voice rang through loud and fucking clear.

Then, grabbing me by the back of the collar of my uniform shirt Cleeve hauled me roughly and meanly to my feet.

"AACCCHHHHHH!!!" I barked the front sections of my shirt and tie pressing hard against my Adam's apple, choking me, the tips of my shoes dangling above the ground as Cleeve hauled me up higher by my shirt collar. "F-fucking bastards!!"

When I was flat on my feet again I quickly took in the sight of the huge mansion-like house sprawled out all by itself on the lonely road.

"WH-what is this place you've brought me to?" I asked, still gasping for air as Cleeve held me by the back of the collar of my uniform shirt.

Before getting a reply to my question though Otis rapped me again good and fucking hard across my pecs with my baton.

"HUUUUFFFFF!!!" I seethed in pain and clenched my teeth in agony as Cleeve held me up by my shirt collar. "UUUURRRHHHHH!!!"

I felt like I was going to choke on my blood if Otis rapped me again that way...

My handcuffs were still dangling off my left wrist, seeing as I had only freed my right wrist while in the trunk.

"This place is my home Officer Stupid," Cleeve said directly into my ear, his tongue grazing and his lips teasing my lobe. "I own everything you see in front of you."

"WH-who are you man? Who the fuck are you?" I whimpered as the two men began hustling me toward the huge house.

"Heh, that's what everyone wants to know," Cleeve responded mockingly. "Come on Otis; let's put him in the woodshed for now. I want to have some warm-up fun before we get to work our new acquisition over..."

"*Son of a fucking bitch...*" I muttered under my breath as they walked me to the back part of the huge house, each of them holding me tightly by one of my arms pulled painfully behind me.

I walked in a wobbly fashion, my knees and thighs aching awfully from the blows they had been dealt, my poor pecs stinging with searing pain as well. When I saw the woodshed where they planned to keep me I struggled mightily, somehow having found a second wind.

"F-FUCKERS!!" I garbled crazily, kicking my legs out as I was moved along. "This is kidnapping!!! And kidnapping a police officer is a federal offense!"

"Yeah, that it is for sure Officer Stupid," Cleeve laughed and the two men hoisted me a few inches off the ground.

They carried me as I continued struggling, my legs kicking out even more-so now as they brought me into the woodshed. Once in the shed they tossed me roughly and bodily against the wooden post that I would soon be trussed to.

"HHHUUFFFFFFFF!!!" I grunted in pain anew as my upper torso connected hard with the post.

I quickly wrapped my arms around the post to keep from falling, my handcuffs dangling mockingly from my wrist. Looking around the woodshed as I turned to face my captors I knew then and there that I was in a shit-load of trouble and that they were not planning on letting me go anytime soon.

"Okay Cop, start stripping," Cleeve said with total authority in his voice as he and Otis stood a few feet away from me, Cleeve holding my gun pointed directly at me. "Down to your shoes and socks..."

I gulped hard and held up a trembling finger...

"N-now look man, kidnapping me is one thing, hauling me into the trunk of your car was downright monstrous and beating on me is going to cost you big fucking time eventually," I said through trembling lips, trying to sound as authoritative as possible and not as terrified as I was actually feeling. "But there is no fucking way that I am going to strip my uniform off for you two perverts!!"

I finished my tirade by spitting on the floor...

With his teeth clenched Cleeve raised my gun, pulled the trigger and the shot was deafening in the small enclosure of the woodshed. I felt the bullet whiz past my head and pass through the small window of the shed, just about missing me.

"*Shit, shit!!!*" I screamed in bloody terror and threw my hands up. "TH-this shit is against the law man!! You're terrorizing a cop here!!"

Still holding the gun pointed at me Cleeve pulled slowly back on the trigger. I nearly shit my pants when I saw that the muzzle of the gun was aimed right between my eyes. I grabbed at my necktie with a quaking hand.

"Strip now Officer Stupid!!" Cleeve said meanly. "Or the next shot you hear will be the last."

"My cop brothers will get you guys for this!!" I whimpered angrily as I undid my necktie.

"The question moreover is will they get you?" Otis asked

me with a grin as I unbuttoned my uniform shirt.

I shucked off my sweat sopped uniform shirt, revealing my bruised and overly muscular barrel-like chest. The two men looked at me lustfully and waving my gun Cleeve pointed at the dusty chair a few feet from where I was standing.

"Take your nameplate and badge off your shirt, hand them to Otis and place your shirt and tie on that chair," Cleeve ordered. "Then get your pants and under shorts off."

With my hands trembling I did as I was told and sadly handed Otis my badge and nametag. Then, I stepped over to the chair and neatly placed my shirt and tie on it. I undid my utility belt and regular belt, placed my utility belt on the chair and facing the two men who had captured me dropped my uniform pants down around my ankles, revealing the fact that I was wearing no under shorts.

"Ha, looks like we got us a freeballing cop," Cleeve laughed. "No under shorts to keep as a souvenir this time Otis."

My cock was rock hard with fear, betraying me and my big juicy plum-like balls hung low in my sexy sac...

Without a word, feeling totally humiliated I bent over to get my uniform pants off over my socks and shoes...I could feel my two captors taking in the sight of my smooth tight bubble butt and my pink bunghole while I was at task of getting my pants off myself...

Cleeve and Otis were licking their lips as I stood straight up and practically at attention before them when I was stripped to my police issued lace-ups and my long black dress socks. They watched with total satisfaction as I placed my pants on the dusty chair along with my shirt and tie.

"Put on your utility belt Cop," Cleeve said to me, the hammer on my gun cocked back.

Doing as the man said I picked up my useless utility belt, slipped it around my naked waist and pre cum oozed and dribbled from my slit, betraying me some more. I breathed heavily...

"Now, get yourself against the post over there, back pressed against it, hands behind you and wrapped around it,"

Cleeve ordered me, my gun pointed now at my head.

"Look, stop this now, *please,*" I said softly, standing there in my almost total nakedness.

Cleeve squeezed the trigger of the gun and without another word I hastily dashed over to the post and positioned myself as he had told me to. My heart felt beyond heavy in my chest as Otis did the honors of re-locking my wrists behind me again in my own handcuffs, around the post. Cleeve held up my handcuff key mockingly.

"Want to try to escape again Officer Stupid?" Cleeve asked me.

I simply pursed my lips together as Otis stepped next to me, looked at me lustfully and grabbed a handful of my big low hanging balls.

"AAAYYYYYYYRRRR" I seethed in pain through clenched teeth. "Fuck man, easy with my balls!!!"

Chuckling, Otis let go of my low hangers and squatted in front of me to get busy roping my feet to the bottom of the post. He used white cotton rope that had been piled near the post, securing my ankles good and tight practically up to my calves, toying with my socks, snapping the elastic in them as he did his work. A few times he stole glances at my pre cum oozing cock...

"Tie him good and tight Otis," Cleeve said. "Officer Stupid isn't going anywhere for some time..."

I looked at Cleeve in utter misery across the woodshed...

When I was tied and cuffed securely to the post Cleeve put my gun down on the chair where my uniform was along with my baton...

The two men stood at my sides looking me over...

"Real good catch Otis," Cleeve said, sounding proud of his buddy. "As always..."

As always? I wondered what that comment meant. Had these two men done this sort of thing before? Had they kidnapped other officers of the law and terrorized them the way they were doing to me, or worse? I wondered if there were reports somewhere in police files on Cleeve and Otis. Somehow I would have to find out, but for the moment I had more pressing issues it would seem. The two men then began running their big mangy hands all over my torso, rubbing my chest roughly, squeezing my nipples hard and twisting the fuck out of them. They reached behind me to grab handfuls of my muscular tight butt cheeks. I literally seethed...

"Fucking perverts!! Get your dirty hands off me you mugs!!" I grunted at them.

"Ha, you ain't in any goddamned position to be telling us what the fuck to do Officer Stupid," Cleeve laughed and gave one of my big man breasts a hard squeezed jiggle, following that up with a hard open handed resounding slap.

"OWWWWWWWWW fuck!!" I spat angrily. "Bad enough you beat on my pecs with my baton, but now you need to be slapping the fucks out of them too?"

While the two men were kneading and mauling me I'm sad to say that my cock was hard and twitching between my tree trunks like legs, my balls churning from the squeeze Otis had given them a few moments before...

Looking down, I watched in horror with my mouth hanging agape as the two men leaned down over my big fleshy man sized tits and slurped one of each of them into their mouths. The sounds of sucking and slurping filled the air in the woodshed as my captors feasted on my man tits.

"AAAAARRRRRRRR fuck, fucking fucks, no, no you guys, I'm no goddamned faggot!" I ranted. "Fucking fuckers, don't be treating my cop tits like a buffet!"

Ignoring me they sucked harder on my tits, nipping at them with their front-most teeth, pulling at the sensitive tips of them with their lips and teeth, seeing how far they could stretch them out on my massive chest. I writhed against the post as chills of agony and ecstasy consumed me, my crotch area jutting out provocatively. My cock was hard and oozing and dribbling small droplets of my cop pre cum.

"FUCKERS, I am going to fuck you mugs up for this!!" I croaked miserably, looking up at the ceiling of the woodshed, not wanting to watch as Cleeve and Otis worked the fuck out of my man tits.

By the time they stopped it was a good (bad?) fifteen to twenty tit torturing minutes later. And...by the time they stopped my man tits were worked up to the size of two ripe cherries jutting out on my chest. Fucking fucks, by the time they stopped my tits were feeling beyond sore, beyond sensitive. GOD, by the time they stopped...

What they did next was unforgivable and shouldn't happen to any cop...

"Give me his badge Otis," Cleeve said.

"WH-what are you mugs up to now?" I seethed as my teeth clenched again. "Don't be fucking with my badge man! That's a cop's prized possession! A cop's badge shows that he's made it!!"

But as I ranted on and on about the merits of a cop's badge Cleeve pulled back the pin on it, tweaked my right sided nipple up to a swollen nub and pinned my badge right onto said nipple, skewering it. "AAAYYYYYYYRRRRRRRRRRRRRR!!!!!" I screamed in bloody agony, looking down at the sudden pain and immense pressure in my poor man tit. "OHHHHHHHHHHHH FFFFUUUUCCCCKKK man, *Oooohhhrrrrrrrrrr GOD, no!!!! YOU bastard!!!*"

The two men looked gleefully with eyes filled with sadism as a thin line of blood crawled down my chest from my newly pierced nipple.

"OHHHHHHHHHRRRR you bastard!! L-Look what the fuck you did to my poor nipple man!! You mutilated it!!" I screamed in Cleeve's face.

"Otis, you can have the honors of doing his nameplate," Cleeve said.

With my eyes still opened wide in terror I turned my head to look at Otis... He was holding my nametag in his hand, the pin on the back of it pulled back.

"You ready Officer Reed?" he asked me and grabbed my left sided nipple in his thumb and first finger.

"OHHHHHH no, no man, please," I pleaded as Otis tweaked my left sided nipple up into a swollen nub, rolling it in his finger and thumb, just as Cleeve had done to my right sided one.

I squeezed my eyes shut tight in utter agony and felt the mean pinch as my nametag skewered my left nipple...

"AAAAYYYYYYRRRRRRRR!!!!" I screamed again in total agony, the sound of my voice filling the woodshed.

Tears streamed from my eyes a few seconds later as the two men took turns squeezing my hard cock and yanking and twisting my low hangers.

"Y-you sick bastards are going to get more than a couple of years behind bars for this shit!!" I ranted in pain, the pressure on my nipples immeasurable to say the least.

"Oh I doubt that very much Officer Stupid," Cleeve said mockingly. "Seeing as you or your cop buddies have no fucking idea where you are. HA!!"

Looking down again I now saw that there were now two thin lines of blood crawling down my muscular chest...

The two men let go of my cock and balls and looked me over for a few seconds. The woodshed was hot as hell and I was a sweaty and grunting mess at that point. Stripped to my shoes and socks and wearing my useless utility belt, my nametag and badge pinned to my damned tits and cinched up in my own handcuffs; fucking fucks, what a sight for a cop of my caliber I thought miserably.

My cock twitched long and fear hard between my legs...

"Come on Otis, lets go relax outside in the sun while Officer Stupid here gets used to his situation," Cleeve said, giving one of my big man breasts a mean hard jiggle.

"Sure thing Cleeve," Otis said, giving my other man breast a hard slap.

"OWWWWWWW!!!" I barked, watching as the two men exited the woodshed, closing and locking the door behind them.

"Fuckers, perverts," I whispered through clenched teeth.

I didn't bother yelling for help, seeing as there was no one around for miles to yell for help from...

So there you have it, there you have the sad narrative of how I came to wind up in this awful predicament...

Then, my thoughts of my capture and early torture were cut short as I heard Otis grunting outside that he was shooting his load now... Fuck, the two men would be coming for me at that point... I just knew it...

"OHHHHHHH yeah, fucking awesome Cleeve," Otis grunted outside in the sun as Cleeve stroked and choked his mess from him, his cum landing all over his massively muscular chest. "Feels great man!!"

Otis' mess of cum on his chest glistened in the sun and Cleeve lovingly licked it from his buddies' chest, swallowing it in greedy gulps, paying special attention to the guy's nipples as he ate the cum off them.

"OHHHHHHHH ea-easy with my tits Cleeve," Otis panted in the afterglow. "You know how fucking sensitive a guy's tits are after he shoots his goddamned big hefty load."

"Sure as shit Otis my man," Cleeve said agreeably. "And you can imagine how the cop's tits must be feeling at this point. When all the cum had been licked off Otis' chest the two men sat side by side on the lounge chair, Otis holding my police radio in hand. He flicked it on and the two men listened.

"Yeah, this is Officer Johnson calling dispatch," they heard through the static, seeing as were obviously out of transmit range. "We've recovered Reed's cruiser and his uniform hat. But no sign of the officer anywhere."

"We roger that Johnson," the female voice at dispatch responded. "We'll put out an APB on Officer Scott Reed. All units in the immediate area to be on the lookout for him."

Otis turned off my radio and the two men laughed heartily and sadistically...

"Immediate area!!" Cleeve's voice boomed. "Immediate fucking area? Fuck, they have no clue just how far out of the immediate area their brother cop is!! Fucking Officer Stupid!! Come on Otis!!"

A few seconds later my heart thundered in my chest as the woodshed door was opened from the outside. The two men stood in the archway in all their muscular glory, clad now in just their thick white sweat socks and work boots. They each had cocks of the meaty and jumbo size; Cleeve's being the meatier, longer and fatter of the two. Their low hanging balls looked like they were bulging and chock filled to overflowing with their man juices. Fuck and they had each shot hefty loads. It looked like these two sadists could go all-day and then some... A thin trickle of after jizz dribbled from Cleeve's cock...

"You ready for us cop?" Cleeve asked as he and Otis entered the woodshed in a predatory like manner.

"Ready for what???" I asked them angrily. "Are you two perverts ready to let me go at this point? You heard my buddy Officer Johnson on the radio. My cop brothers are out there searching for me at this very moment."

"Sure as shit they are," Cleeve said and he and Otis sidled up to my sides, jiggling my nametag and badge on my poor tortured man tits, sending chills of searing pain through me. "But I seriously doubt that they'll be coming here looking for you. HA!!!!!"

"OWWWWWWRRRR!!!" I grunted and arched my crotch area forward; my hard as a flagpole cock swinging outward as the two men pulled and tugged on my nametag and badge, causing indescribable pain to shoot through the thin skin of my cop tits. "Don't you two bet on it man! When a cop is missing they'll search fucking high and low till he's found... OWWWWWWRRRR SHHHHIIITTTTT!!!!"

"This cop cock of yours got hard waiting for us?" Otis asked me mockingly, reaching down and giving my low hangers a tight squeeze and hard cock a twirl, sending droplets of my pre cum splattering to the floor.

"I fucking doubt that," I seethed in his face and involuntarily gyrated my crotch area. "As I told you mugs, I'm no damned faggot!!"

Smiling meanly Otis slowly slid to his knees in front of me, wrapped his hands around the top-most part of my long socks and slurped my hard crusted cock into his mouth.

"OHHHHHHHHHH oh no, oh no, oh no, not this you perverts," I grunted in a mixture of ecstasy and out-right humiliation. "OH GAWD, don't be sucking my cock man!!"

Standing beside me Cleeve took my badge in hand and undid the pin skewering my nipple that it was hanging on.

"WH-what are you doing man?" I asked him through trembling lips.

Slowly, Cleeve slid my badge off my nipple, the pain coursing through my nub sending chills of pain through my being.

"AAAAAYYYYYYRRRR fuck, my poor tits!!" I seethed with tears in my eyes.

Looking down as Cleeve got my badge off my nipple I watched in disbelief as Otis sucked my crusty hardness for all he was worth, giving my low hanging sweaty balls a few tugs and squeezes every few seconds.

"OOOHHHRRRRR GOD, GOD of gods, I do not fucking believe this you mugs, but I'm getting close here," I panted madly, arching my crotch area sexily forward. "I'm goin' to shoot a real cop-sized load of spunk here you bastards!! Fuck, got me sweatin' in my socks!!"

Droplets of blood oozed to the tip of my nipple that Cleeve had just taken my badge off of. I blanched and nearly passed out when he sucked my bleeding nipple into his mouth and chowed the fuck on it.

"OHHHHHHHRRRR fuck, wh-what are you, some kind of blood sucking vampire pervert?" I asked the guy, but then my words were cut short as I felt myself shooting my load, right into Otis's mouth, right down his gullet. "AAAAARRRRRRHHHHH sshhhhhiiiiittt, lookit this shit, fucking cop kidnappers got me cummin' like goddamned gangbusters!!!"

I balled my cuffed hands into a tight fist and sweating like crazy arched my head back against the post. Otis went on and on sucking the fuck out of my manhood, gulping down my mess each time I erupted.

"OOOOOOHHHHRRRR p-perverts, eating my cum and sucking the blood from my damned tit, I seethed.

Otis's tongue was like magic as it swirled around my spurting cock. I again arched my crotch area forward, looked down, saw how my cock was impaled in Otis's mouth and let fly with another good strand of my good stuff.

"UUUUHHHHHHHH..." I grunted as Otis scoffed down that eruption as well.

When I couldn't cum anymore Otis got to his feet and standing beside me took my nametag in hand. Cleeve stopped sucking my bloody tit momentarily and watched as Otis did with my nametag what he had done just moments before with my badge. Otis undid the pin holding my nametag to my pierced tit and slowly slid the needle off it.

"AAAAAYYYYRRRRRfuuuuuucccckkkkkkk!!!!"I screeched throatily.

"Like I said Cleeve, a guy's tits are always sensitive after he shoots a good-sized load," Otis said.

"Sure as shit," Cleeve replied and took my low hangers in hand, squeezing them. "And from the way these balls of his are feeling all hefty he's going to be beyond sensitized by the time we get done with him today..."

The two men chuckled meanly; they both leaned down then over my chest and greedily slurped one of my bleeding tits each into their mouths...

The sounds of my agony mixed with forced ecstasy filled the small woodshed and the scent of sweat and cum assaulted my nostrils as the two men ate my cop tits with utter gusto. It was a horrid feeling as they sucked and chewed on them and I felt the blood oozing from them. I swear it was like a psycho nursing baby was on my goddamned tits.

Later, Cleeve and Otis exited the woodshed a second time, leaving me handcuffed and roped at the feet to the post still, this time blindfolded as well...

"We'll be back again real soon Officer Stupid," Cleeve called out to me from the door of the woodshed.

I heard the door of the shed pulled closed and locked. I silently thanked God that they hadn't pinned my nametag and badge back to my poor swollen and wounded cop tits...

"Come on Otis, lets let Officer Reed get his energy back," I heard Cleeve saying. "In the meantime we'll check on that slave of ours down in the shaving room..."

My mouth dropped open in out-right horror at what I had just heard Cleeve say... A slave in a shaving room???

What had I fallen into here???

Who was Cleeve? Who was Otis? What the fucking fuck was to become of me???

I leaned the back of my head against the post and cried big tears of fear behind my cloth blindfold...

The End

Author's After-word

The short story "Captured Cop" was inspired by various factors. It amazes me how an eleven page story could have so many influences and inspirations...

Originally the story was dedicated to a past AOL buddy of mine named Scott. Scott had a severe fetish for wearing his business suits to work with no underpants on underneath his suit trousers. The word for this particular fetish is "Freeballing." It was because of Scott that I named the captured police officer in the story "Scott." (The reason for the cop's last name "Reed" will be explained in detail shortly.) It was also because of Scott and his request that when the cop in the story is stripped down to his socks and shoes that it be revealed that he is not wearing any underpants, that he is "Freeballing" in his uniform, as Scott had so aptly stated it. Over the years I lost contact with Scott but the story will live on...

To sum it up the story chronicles in very quick detail a police officer's worst nightmare, of being abducted by not just one but two crazed lunatics, and in this case, who better than my two crazed recurring characters, Cleeve and Otis...

Cleeve and Otis made their first appearance in a segment of my fictional memoir, "Greg Smith- Episodes of my Life." At the time of that writing Cleeve and Otis were meant to be only support characters in that particular story. But as time went on I decided to give Cleeve and Otis their own series of stories. They were so villainous in their appearance in the "Greg Smith" story that I felt they deserved more recognition. I also felt that readers of my work could get some good insights into just what these two unique characters were capable of... It also gave readers a peek into my darker side of writing as well... It was determined in "Greg Smith- Episodes of my Life" that these two rugged and brawny men were always on the prowl in the wee morning hours for what they called "male marks" that they could use for their sadistic antics. In the Cleeve and Otis stories that I went on to write it was determined that after they abducted and worked over their latest "male mark", the man was released within twenty-four hours time of his abduction, usually. Greg Smith was an exception, seeing as he was, in Cleeve's words, "something to really hold onto." In "Captured Cop" Cleeve and Otis hold onto the cop and at the story's end it is never determined when they will release him...if at all... Cleeve's mention of the slave they have in their shaving room is a direct (and yes, deliberate) plug to my story, "Larry, Captured by Cleeve and Otis." This story, "Captured Cop", is also one of the rarities where we see Cleeve and Otis being affectionate to each other in a sexual sense. This surprised me, especially as the author, seeing as Cleeve and Otis always maintain that they are straight and that the only reason they hunt and captured men is that men fight and resist a lot better than women do. It is also the first story where Cleeve uses a gun to terrorize a mark. In this case he uses the captured cop's confiscated service revolver. This story shows a rawer, more primal side of Cleeve.

The character of Officer Scott Reed in the story "Captured Cop" was largely and nearly directly influenced by Officer Jim Reed (although the cop's first name of Scott as I mentioned was because of my AOL buddy Scott) from the 1970's TV cop series, "Adam-12", who was portrayed to perfection by actor Kent McCord... (If you're wondering why I named the leather master "Kent" in my story "The Taking of Master's Boy" now you know.) As my buddy Joe T. once said "Officer Jim Reed was the handsomest cop ever in TV history. In the episode of "Adam-12", entitled "Trouble at the Bank" Officer Jim Reed is taken hostage by two bank robbers when he unwittingly walks into a robbery-in-process. One of the men who capture Officer Reed is named Cleeve, although in the TV episode his name is spelled "Cleave." When I first saw that episode years ago the name "Cleeve" just stuck in my head for whatever the reason. I guess it just sounds like a name for a really mean guy, no offense to any guys out there named Cleeve. Or maybe I somehow knew that I would be using the name for a fictional character of my own at some point down the line...

The opening scene of "Captured Cop" where Officer Reed is cinched to the post in the woodshed while Cleeve and Otis are outside enjoying themselves in the sun I admit that I lifted directly from the Zeus video "Ranch Slave Trainee." In that video's opening sexy Canadian porn actor and lanky muscle boy Jimmy Dean (no, not that Jimmy Dean) is seen tied up to a post in a woodshed, his hands cinched behind him and his booted feet cinched to the bottom of the post, keeping him balanced and in place. The tied up actor is clad in no more than his boots and a pair of ripped up denim short shorts with his cock and balls dangling out the side of them. While Jimmy Dean struggles to get untied and swears under his breath over his bondage plight, his two captors porn actors James DeFalco and Mark Saber (I believe those were the actors in that video) are outside in the sun enjoying each other sexually. I decided on Cleeve and Otis to be the kidnappers in my story "Captured Cop" rather than two new characters when I saw the Zeus video. The reason for Cleeve and Otis's affection toward each other for the first time is explained in the opening scenes of the Zeus video, seeing as I very much wanted to mirror that. Even the way Officer Scott Reed struggles to get free mirrors Jimmy Dean's gyrations in the video. Like James DeFalco and Mark Saber in the video Cleeve and Otis are extremely muscular, very sadistic, yet very attractive men. In the video "Ranch Slave Trainee" it is never explained how Jimmy Dean came to be tied up in the woodshed. If one ponders it long enough it could be that his two captors nabbed him when he was hitchhiking. It is possible that he could even be a captured police officer of some kind, like in my story. Jimmy Dean saying "You gonna let me go or what?" as James DeFalco and Mark Saber enter the woodshed explains that he has been captured and is an unwilling mark in their sadistic game of sexual torture…

At some point down the line I will more than likely write a sequel or two for "Captured Cop" but for the moment I think it stands pretty well on its own…

Happy Reading…

Christopher Trevor

The Burglar

A note from the author: *The following story was inspired by the artist Dom Orejudos, otherwise known as Stephen and also known as Etienne, Etienne being French for the name Stephen. His drawn story "Forced Entry" was very inspirational in bringing ex Air Force flyboy Trevor Stevens and his captor, a sinister burglar, known only as Mike to life in my story "The Burglar." Etienne, as I will always remember him named was born on July 1st, 1933 and I must say that no other artist (other than Tom of Finland and Joe T) has ever inspired my work like his did. Etienne painted astonishing 8 to 10 foot giants of oil and acrylic works, giving homage to mythical men of might and unusual brawn, hence the way Trevor Stevens in my following tale is able to shoot his load umpteen times when captured and accosted by Mike the burglar. Although, while it goes without saying in the story Mike the burglar is mysteriously adept at using terror to somehow arouse his unwitting prisoner. Like in the horrifically suspenseful movie "The Hitcher" (starring C. Thomas Howell and Rutger Hauer) we the audience sense some sort of love story emerging between the victim and his tormentor. Etienne will go down in homoerotic history, of that I have no doubt at all, as being the quintessential humorist. His typical drawings and storylines usually had one or more characters as the brunt of the evil joke, many times under severe physical torment, in bondage most times and all for the gratification of another of his villains or ruffians if you would. His vivid imagination created the finest looking men, with an overabundance of testosterone and male pheromones and then spiraled those men into the most bizarre situations. His artwork helped to release the sides of ourselves that have a fascination with erotic danger, sometimes inviting it, fulfilling it within the* scopes of our imaginations. My story "The Burglar" was inspired as I said by Etienne's drawn story "Forced Entry" wherein a handsome muscular guy sleeping in his apartment is captured and accosted by an intruder. In "Forced Entry" there were two intruders who got the drop on a hunky construction worker. In my story "The Burglar" there is one only one intruder who manages to capture and make into a sexual slave of sorts and the butt of his sinister humor the handsome executive he finds sleeping in the apartment he is currently ransacking. I paid tribute to Etienne by having the burglar find out that the handsome executive he captures was once in the Air Force. Etienne's fascination with military uniforms came into play here when the burglar forces the executive to don his old military uniform and then proceeds to brutally rape the guy while clad in his uniform of honor and high-standing. Nothing can be more humiliating for a military man, at least in my opinion. I might be taking artistic license there, I don't really know. My own fetish for dress socks was mixed in as well when the burglar finds the executive sleeping and wearing his leftover dress socks from the previous workday. Like me, Etienne had an erotic fascination with men who wore black dress socks. Various pieces of his work and stories attest to this and a collection was once done featuring Etienne's men wearing black socks. On his deathbed Etienne wanted all his fans (myself being an avid one) to be aware that he in no way wanted them to actualize any of the situations that he had created in his drawings, for it is make believe, just as I have pointed out where my sinister and erotic stories are concerned. So with all this in mind I thank the Tom of Finland organization for keeping Etienne's works around for us to enjoy and fantasize over, I thank Durk Dehner for his commentary on Etienne and I thank Joe T. the artist who I was lucky enough to meet in person and have dinner with numerous times for introducing me to the exceptional and unique works of the man known as "Etienne." Without Etienne a lot of my own stories would not have come to life…

Happy Reading…
Christopher Trevor

The Story

I had been a fool. I had been utterly and completely stupid. I had been had. I had left the window open and the shade up in my bedroom because it was a warm evening in June, early summer. Not hot enough yet to use the air conditioner but warm enough to leave the window open wide. As I said, I had been a complete and stupid fool. Because now I was lying trapped on my own bed. I was lying on my stomach in a miserably uncomfortable hog-tied position. (My arms were pulled back behind me and roped tightly at the wrists with mounds of rope. My blue dress socked feet were pulled back and roped off at the ankles to my wrists. A quadruple set of tit clamps was on my nipples and the other side of them was clamped to my bed sheets, holding me awfully in place. Every time I tried to raise myself the fucking tit clamps pulled harshly on my poor nubs, threatening to rip them off my big muscular chest. What a fucked up position to be in, and in my own apartment no less.) He had climbed up the fire escape to my second floor apartment unseen by anyone at one thirty AM that morning. I was sleeping soundly as the big husky burglar climbed silently through my open window. Stupid of me, it was as if I had invited the bastard in. He had come with the intention of simply ripping me off. And what New York burglar could pass up the chance at an open window during the night? And what New York burglar could ignore an open window with a fire escape right outside it and only two stories up no less. For a New York City burglar that was all easy pickings let me tell you. But then by the light of the moon shining in my window he saw *me* sleeping there. I was on my back lying atop the covers, clad in just my left over navy blue dress socks from the workday before and a pair of white briefs. My body is muscular and rippled and in my sleep I heard a deep intake of breath when the guy caught sight of me. I stirred slightly in my sleep as the guy silently put his large backpack on the floor. He stealthily made his way over to my bed, drinking me in, devouring me with his eyes. My big pink nipples were erect on my muscular chest as it rose and fell with my breaths. My dick was semi hard in my briefs. My big juicy balls pressed against the cotton material of my briefs, outlining themselves for him to see. My wallet was on my dresser my gold chains were on my night table. All the bastard had to do was grab those things and be on his fucking way. But no, I had to be lying there all decked out and real sexy looking in my sleep for him. He closed the window and the sound of the window hitting the sill roused me from slightly from my sleep.

"Mmmmm..." I murmured with my eyes closed. "Wha wasss that?"

"Just me you gorgeous fucking stud!!" he said and grabbed a handful of my wavy brown hair.

"*Huh?*" I gasped, coming fully and awkwardly awake then.

Before I could do anything the bastard yanked me off my bed by my hair.

"Yaaaahhhhrrrrr!!!!" I roared as I was pulled off the bed and to my socked feet.

He was just about the same height as I, six feet two to three inches tall, but not as muscular and built as I. Still, the bastard had the advantage of surprise over me.

"Uhhhhhfffff, who, who the fuck're you?" I gasped as he held me tightly by my hair and danced me around my room on my socked feet. "F-fuckin' burglar...HOLY FUCKING SHIT!!!"

"Hate to do this to you bud but I need to take some of the fight out of you," he said meanly as I clenched my hands into fists, ready to do battle with the invading fucker.

Because I was still groggy with sleep my reflexes were down. He made a fist and punched me hard, super fucking hard square in the gut.

"Hoooooofffff!!!!" I sputtered and practically jumped out of my blue calf length socks as the pain shot through me at what seemed like a hundred miles an hour.

He held tightly to my hair as I tried in vain to struggle out of his grasp, yanking me to my toes. Then, he made another fist and punched me hard again, square in the old gut.

"Hoooooofffff!!!!" I gasped again and doubled over in pain, coughing and gagging miserably.

Still holding me by the handful of my hair the bastard walked me doubled over and in pain quickly toward a wall. He let go of my hair, sending me flying against the wall. The top of my head hit the wall and I hit the floor on my knees.

"Ohhhhh good God," I moaned miserably.

My reflexes and my Air force training were completely useless to me at that moment. The bastard had the drop on me and he was taking full advantage of it. Soon he would be taking full advantage of me.

"Okay Gorgeous on your feet!!" he said meanly from behind me.

Again he grabbed a handful of my wavy brown hair, hauled me to my feet, whirled me around, and slammed me bodily against the wall, facing him.

"Wh-who are you?" I gasped and took another hard punch to the gut. "OOOOOfffff!!!! *Bastard!!*"

"Just your friendly neighborhood burglar handsome guy," he said fiendishly. "But it looks like this time I'm going to get a little more than just money, jewelry and other odds and ends that you well to do business guys in this neighborhood keep around the house."

I had heard the stories in the neighborhood of people being robbed while they were asleep during the night. Where I lived in Manhattan was a neighborhood comprised mostly of business executives, company vice presidents, office managers and some business owners as well. People had reported waking up in the morning to find numerous valuable items gone; their place ransacked all while they had slept. Couples were astound-ed that they had slept through being robbed. One big burly guy was totally pissed off seeing as his wife was a very sexy woman, as he made clear in a TV news interview. He said that had the burglar decided to kill him he could have had his way with his beautiful wife and perhaps killed her too. It was clear that most people, especially the elderly and single women who lived alone were terrified at the thought of someone being in their apartment while they slept. We had a neighborhood meeting on a Saturday afternoon and everyone agreed to be on the lookout for anyone who seemed suspicious, threatening or out of place in any way. But hell, this was New York. In New York a lot of people seem out of place. While at that waste of time neighborhood meeting I never for a second thought that I could wind up in the burglar's clutches and be used in the ways he used me. There were no stories of the burglar raping any of his victims, especially the men he robbed. He hadn't touched any of the beautiful women he had robbed so everyone took a slight comfort in the fact that he was just a cat burglar. RIGHT! Because now he was in my apartment and he had gotten the drop on me. And based on his comment of getting more than just money and jewelry from me sent me into a rage.

"You're a slimy faggot!!" I grunted and again clenched my fists.

But alas, I was in no position to try to get the advantage over him. The bastard was fast, that was for sure. This time he gave my nuts a good hard whack.

"Arrrrrrrhhhh!!!!" I roared in total agony and crumpled to the floor at his booted feet, my hands over my crotch. "*You fucking low life bastard!!*"

Chuckling fiendishly and meanly he *again* grabbed a handful of my hair and pulled me only halfway to my feet this time. I felt a wave of defeat overwhelm me.

"L-look, take what you want and get the hell out of here!!" I grunted, looking down at the floor as he held me by my hair.

"Ah, but it's not as cut and dry as that handsome guy," he said and tugged on my thick mustache. "You see, when I came through that window and saw you I decided I wanted more than just your possessions and whatever money you got stashed in that wallet over there."

With that he yanked a few hairs from my thick mustache and as I screamed miserably in pain he hauled me bodily across the room. I landed on my back with my socked feet flat on the floor and my legs spread. Stupid of me for sure. Damn, but I was taking a real fucking beating from the guy. He quickly made his way over to me, grabbed my socked ankles, and lifted me in an upside down position off the floor.

"Uhhhhrrrrr, bastard, put me the fuck down!!" I grunted, my arms flailing uselessly out at my sides.

"Heh heh, your wish is my command handsome guy," he chortled and dropped me.

I landed on the floor head first, a stupor taking me away...

"OOOOffff..." I muttered stupidly.

As I lay there he made his way over to the backpack that he had dropped on the floor when he came through my window. He opened the backpack as I rolled over onto my back and saw him taking rope out of it.

"Going to have to tie you up for a while handsome guy," he said, coming back over to me with the rope hanging around his neck.

He took me by my upper arms and dragged me toward my bed. Suddenly, utter rage consumed me and I felt a second wind inside me. I *would not allow this!!* I would not be roped up and taken prisoner in my own damned apartment. I came out of the stupor I had been knocked into and pulled violently away from him.

"Uhhhnnffff..." I grunted as I stumbled away from him.

"Shit!!" he bellowed angrily.

"Okay man, now you either get the fuck out of my apartment or I'm going to make short work of you!!" I said, trying to sound as threatening as possible while standing there in just my socks and briefs. "I recently completed four years of service in the United States Air Force and believe you me I'm more than well trained in hand to hand combat!"

I clenched my fists and assumed a fighter's stance, slightly shaking from the punches and blows I'd been dealt. Inside myself I knew I wasn't kidding anybody. I was in no position to be fighting someone smaller than I, let alone a burglar of about my size. With lightning fast speed he reached out and grabbed one of my wrists. The fucker had the strength of a bull that was for sure, HOLY FUCK! He yanked me toward him, me sliding stupidly on my socked feet.

"Ufffffff, shit!!!" I gasped and suddenly there was a knife being held just mere inches from my throat.

"Not a move you gorgeous stud," he said meanly, slightly pressing the tip of the blade against my Adam's apple. "Looks like all that Air Force training is really coming in handy now."

"Shit, shit, shit," I gasped miserably at having him get the drop on me again.

He let go of my wrist and my hands automatically went up at my sides and above my head.

"Pl-please man, I don't know what you have in mind," I said through trembling lips, shaking in total fear in my socks at that moment. "J-just don't kill me man, please, please don't kill me!"

Holding the knife at my throat with one hand he gave one of my big pink nipples a squeeze with his other hand.

"Get over to the bed guy," he said with authority in his voice.

I backed slowly toward the bed as he held the knife under my throat my hands still raised. I was choking back tears of fear, rage, and humiliation. When I was standing next to the bed he turned me away from him. Holding the knife at my throat he put an arm around me from behind, pulling me close to him, a hand cupping the bottom of one of my big man breasts, his thumb pressed against my big pink nipple. A chill went through me as I felt his hard-on pressing against my ass through his black jeans and my white briefs. He rubbed my nipple tip with his thumb and my breath caught in my throat.

"Bring your hands down slowly and cross them behind you at the wrists handsome guy," he said, moving the knife away from my throat.

"L-look, you don't have to tie me up," I began to say,

but then I felt the tip of the knife against the center of my back. *"Shit..."*

I did as he said, slowly bringing my hands behind me and crossing them at the wrists. Quickly, he wound rope around and around my crossed wrists, binding my hands tightly behind me. I stood there with my head slightly thrown back, a look of utter defeat and shame etched on my square-jawed face. When my hands were securely roped behind me he seemed to relax a little, knowing that he now had me totally at his mercy. I felt the tip of the knife moving over the seat of my briefs, down the crack of my ass, over the waistband of them. He did this over and over to me, numerous times, caressing me with the sharp tip of the knife, gliding it over and over my briefs.

"Oh God, what are you going to do to me?" I asked him, choking on my tears.

"Well, for starters you won't be needing these cute little briefs of yours," he said and slit the side of my briefs with his knife.

The sound of the cotton material being slashed filled my ears. When I looked down and saw him working the knife over the crotch area of my briefs I held my breath. The tip of the knife just barely brushed the tip of my semi hard dick as it cut my briefs off me. I was left with the just the elastic waistband of my briefs, the rest of them in tatters on the floor at my feet. He moved the palm of a big hand over my bulging biceps, over my chest, and over my nipples as he stood behind me holding me close to him, his crotch pressed against my naked ass now.

"Ohhhhh man, you really are a fucking gorgeous stud," he said and grabbed a handful of my big juicy balls. "Looks like I've struck gold this time."

He held my balls tight, squeezing them, inflicting pain.

"Pl-please man," I squeaked as he moved the knife over my eight-inch dick. *"Please don't, oh good God, please don't!!"*

Snickering, he took the knife away from my dick and let go of my balls. He stepped a few inches away from me and I could feel his eyes moving over me from behind.

"Oooooo yeah, I'm really going to have fun with you," he said breathlessly and gave my coconut shaped ass cheeks a hard open-handed slap.

"Yowwwchhhh!!!" I growled.

"Turn around and face me you fucking gorgeous stud," he commanded.

Not having much choice in the matter I did as I was told, trembling in my socks, and slowly turning around to face him. My wide shoulders were thrown back as I practically stood there at attention before him. My dick was semi hard in front of me. It was oozing droplets of cum and piss. I had been asleep for a while so like most guys it stood to reason that the need to piss was setting in.

"Looks like you're enjoying all this Stud," he said mockingly, giving my dick a quick pull.

When I nodded "no" he reeled around and gave me a hard whack across the side of my head. It sent me backward onto my bed. I lay there in a stupor again as he positioned me on my stomach and pulled my socked feet up behind me toward my bound hands...

"As soon as I've got you all hog-tied and helpless I have another surprise waiting for you in my backpack," he said as he roped my socked feet to my hands at the ankles. "And I honestly don't think you're going to like it Stud."

I scrunched my eyes closed and heard the sounds of him sniffing the bottoms of my smelly socked feet.

"Pervert," I whispered as tears seeped out of the sides of my tightly closed eyes.

When he was done tying me he pressed his nose and mouth against the bottom of one of my blue-socked feet and inhaled deeply.

"Mmmm... tell me guy, what size are these smelly feet of yours?" he asked me and snapped the elastic in one of my socks against my calf.

"El-eleven," I stammered as spittle flew out of my mouth and I felt his tongue moving over the bottom of one of my feet.

"Fucking pervert, licking my damned smelly feet!!"

I wriggled my toes angrily under my socks as the guy reached under me and brought my big dick and juicy balls out from under me. I shuddered uncontrollably as goose bumps crept all over me as he handled my manhood. Surprisingly I was fear-hard and pulsing.

"Heh heh, oh yeah, now I know what to do to you next," he said and climbed off the bed.

I watched helplessly as he walked again over to his back-pack on the floor. He reached into it and brought out a quadruple set of tit clamps, meaning that there were four clamps on the thin short chain rather than just two. The ways I was tied in that hog-tie my nipples were completely vulnerable and visible for what he had in mind. I shuddered as he positioned himself in front of me. I watched in tortured agony as he clamped two of the clamps to the sheet on the bed just under my nipples.

"Oh *no*" I gasped hoarsely.

Then, he stretched the short chain with the other two clamps toward my waiting nipples.

"Am I going to have to gag you for this guy?" he asked me, the tit clamps open and waiting around my poor nipples. "I really don't want to attract any unnecessary attention. I truly want you all to myself, that's how much you mean to me, HA! I'm just glad no one heard me throwing you that beating."

I shook my head "no" and he closed the clamps tightly onto my nipples. They pulled my poor nipples down hard and toward the bed sheet.

"RRRRRhhhhhh!!!!" I seethed through clenched teeth. "Fuck man, why don't you just rob me and get it over with already?"

"Oh you handsome bastard, I have a lot more than just robbing you in mind," he said gleefully yet meanly. "We're going to get to know each other real well before I'm out of here."

Smiling down at me, his dark eyes gleaming he cupped my chin in his hand, stroked it gently, and stood up again. Looking up at him I quickly took in the fact that he had curly dark hair, dark eyes, and a goatee. I guessed his age to be in the early to mid twenties. Younger than I by a few years at least. He moved back behind me and I heard him spit a few times into his hand. Then, with his slicked with saliva hand he took my hard pulsing dick in a tight grip. "Ohhhhhh fuck, what're you doin' man?" I blurted as he began slowly stroking my big dick. "I'm not a damned faggot!!"

"No need to be a faggot to shoot your wad a few times and then some," he said to me, stroking me a little faster. "I'm going to milk you every half hour you handsome fuck. By the time a few hours have past you'll be shooting dry loads, and believe you me, by then I'll have to have gagged you because that shit can drive a guy crazy. Instead of screaming in ecstasy you're going to be screaming in total agony. Tell me something handsome guy, did you ever jack off so much as a teenager that after a while you were shooting dry loads? HA! I don't know why but for some fucked up reason that can make a poor sap of a guy go crazy."

"Ohhhhh shit, you perverted bastard!!" I grunted as chills crept through me as he stroked me and stroked me and stroked me some more. "ohhhhh man, getting close already you slimy fuck!!"

"I would guess that you haven't gotten off in a while then huh handsome guy?" he asked me mockingly and stroked me faster and faster. "Saving it up for your girlfriend for when you see her over the weekend I'll bet. HA, all you handsome silk socked office boys save it for the girlfriend all week. You're all too busy trying to impress your bosses from Monday to Friday. Then on the weekends you plow your pretty ladies like they were fields. But not this time you gorgeous stud, this time you'll be giving those loads to me!!"

As he sat on my bed behind me stroking the fuck out of my big dick he ran his lips over the side of one of my socked feet, sending more chills through me.

"Fuck man, seems to me like you got a thing for those big smelly feet of mine eh?" I asked him breathlessly as I felt myself getting ready to shoot a real hefty sized load of ball juice.

"Oh yeah, every part of you is real appetizing looking you

handsome fuck," he said and stole a suck at one of my socked toes.

"Ohhhh, yeah, I-I'm fucking cumming now you bastard!!" I grunted, feeling my dick come totally alive and tingle in his hand. "Ohhhhhh God, yeahhhh!!!"

He stroked me hard, pumping every possible drop of cum from me. I spurted madly onto the sheets beneath me, shooting ropes upon ropes of creamy man juice. I grunted miserably as the tit clamps tugged hard on my nipples as I tried to move around on the bed. He was still stroking me.

"Ohhh fuck, can't believe this shit has happened to me!!" I panted.

When I was done shooting what would be the first of many loads that night he let go of my dick. It landed hard in the puddle of my cum that was all over the sheet. I stupidly thought how I and my girlfriend were going to have to go shopping to get me some new sheets, JEEZ! Then, my nipples were in total agony, cutting off any rational thoughts for the moment. I buried my face in the pillow, screamed loudly, and muffled. I had just discovered just how sensitive a guy's nipples become after having just shot a hefty sized load of ball juice. Having a pair of clamps fastened tightly to them made it even worse. Agonizing pain and stinging chills coursed through me at what felt like a hundred fucking miles per hour.

"Ohhhhhhhh GAWD take these fucking things off my nips you bastard!!" I screamed muffled into the pillow. "God almighty, I will kill you for this shit!!"

After a short while the pain eased up somewhat. The guy turned the lamp on my night table on, pulled down the shade on my window, and pulled a chair that I kept in the bedroom up along side my bed.

"Now, what say you and I get to know each other a little," he said, sitting down on the chair and propping his booted feet up on the bed next to me. "We have a half hour to kill before I milk that juicy cock of yours again."

I looked at him miserably and in utter rage.

"That's what you're goin' to do to me man???" I blurted, feeling totally humiliated and violated. "You're going to stay here and milk my damned cock over and over? Fuck man, I don't need you to do that for me…"

"I said lets get to know each other man, unless you want a face full of the bottom of my boot that is," he said and I had awful visions of him kicking me in the face, knocking my teeth out.

I clammed up for the moment…

"Okay, I'll start, my name is Mike," he said, folding his arms over his big chest and smiling at me. "And you are?"

He was wearing a black tee shirt with black jeans. His black work boots were a few inches from my face, close enough to do real damage if he decided to kick outwards.

"M-my name is Trevor, Trevor Stevens" I replied.

"Nice to meet you Trevor Stevens," he snickered. "I would shake your hand but you're a little tied up at the moment.

He laughed hysterically at his stupid joke.

"L-look man, what do you want?" I asked him.

"You already know that handsome guy," he replied.

"B-but I'm not gay," I responded in utter misery. "Pl-please stop this."

"No can do handsome guy," he said and pressed the tip of one of his boots against my chin. "You mesmerize me. Now, lick."

Oh jeez," I seethed.

With no choice other than to do as I was told I stuck out my tongue and licked the tip of his work boot a few times. The smell of leather and dung filled my mouth.

"So, tell me Trevor Stevens, what do you do for work?" he asked me, mockingly trying to make conversation.

"I'm an account executive with a bank in Manhattan," I replied.

"Ah, but you mentioned Air Force training handsome guy," he said to me.

"I-I did four years in the Air Force after I graduated high school," I explained.

"Fat lot of good your basic training did you where I'm concerned Trevor ol' boy," he snickered meanly.

I pursed my lips and looked at him blankly.

"Fucker, you got the jump on me," I retorted angrily. "Wasn't a fair fucking fight!!"

"I'm robbing you handsome guy, I didn't have time for a fair fucking fight," he said and again pressed the tip of one of his boots against my chin. "Lick."

I worked up some saliva in my mouth to get my tongue good and wet and again licked his black leather boot. As I did so I felt my dick getting hard in the puddle of my cum. When he pulled his foot away from me he stood up and looked around my bedroom.

"Nice bedroom you have here handsome guy," he said. "You decorate all this yourself?"

"I-I had a little help," I replied.

He stepped over to my night table and picked up the five by seven framed picture of my girlfriend and I.

"She's pretty," he said, running the tip of a finger over the picture in which my girlfriend was dressed in a print dress and I was in a dark blue business suit. "What's her name?"

"Y-you leave her alone!!" I seethed angrily through clenched teeth, managing to raise my head a few inches up off the bed, looking at him as he trailed his finger over my side of the picture. "If you touch her I swear that when I'm out of this *I will find you and I will kill you!!*"

"Relax handsome guy, it's not her I'm interested in," he said. "As far as I'm concerned you're first prize here."

"Shit, of all things," I muttered.

"What's her name?" he asked me again.

"Linda," I replied and lay my head back down on the bed.

"In Spanish that means beautiful," he said.

Then, he swung the picture back and rammed it against the pointed edge of my night table, shattering the glass frame. Bits and pieces of glass flew across the room and some landed on the floor.

"H-hey man," I grunted. "Wh-what're you doing? There was no need to do that!"

"Just preparing the first of a few souvenirs of this little venture!" he replied somewhat angrily.

He pulled the picture of Linda and I out of the frame, dropped the frame on the floor, and tore the picture down the middle. The side with Linda's picture in it he dropped to the floor along with the shards of the ruined frame. The side with my picture in it he crammed into a back pocket of his black jeans. Shit, I thought miserably. That picture had sentimental value to me. A waiter in a restaurant took it of us on the night of Linda's and my second date. After we had met at a business seminar I had asked Linda if she would have dinner with me some time. She had said yes. After that date I called a day later and asked if she would have dinner with me again. When she said yes a second time I considered myself to be the luckiest son of a bitch in the world. She had brought a camera along and asked our waiter to take a picture of us all dressed up on our second date. I kept that picture on my night table since getting it. Now this faggot burglar had decided that he was hot for me and wanted my picture as a damned souvenir!

"How long have you been dating this Linda?" he asked, sounding almost disgusted.

"A-about five or six months now," I replied and watched as he leaned down and opened the bottom drawer of my night table, my sock drawer to be exact. Smiling, he reached in and brought out a box of condoms.

"Heh heh, all you fucking so called straight guys keep your rubbers in your damned sock drawer," he snickered and dropped the box on the floor.

"I am not a *so-called* straight guy!!" I roared at him. "*I am straight!! And this is a fucking shitty thing you're doing to me!!*"

"By the time I'm done with you tonight handsome guy you'll be begging me to come here every night and tie you the fuck up for a while!" he said and knelt on my bed by my raised and tied feet.

I wished he would stop calling me handsome guy, it really grated on my hyped up nerves let me tell you. I shuddered as he wrapped his hands around my calves, leaned down, and pressed his nose and mouth against the bottoms of my socked feet.

"Mmmm, smells so good these feet of yours," he said in ecstasy. "These smelly socks of yours will make a good souvenir too. I'll take them too when this is over, but that's hours and hours from now handsome guy."

He chuckled meanly and sniffed heartily at my socked feet, running the palms of his hands up and down and up and down my calves. Like most office guys out there I tend to leave my socks on after climbing out of the monkey suit after reaching home. I don't know why I do it, just that it's some sort of guy thing I suppose.

"Look man, as you can see I have a whole fucking drawer filled with socks," I said miserably. "You can fucking have them all for all I care. Just rob me, untie me, and *please get the fuck out of here already!!"*

Ignoring me he slurped at my socked toes and squeezed my calves tighter and tighter. Chills slithered through me as he sucked at my toes and my dick grew harder under me. God almighty what the fuck was that all about?

"So Trevor Stevens, do you like what you do for a living at that bank you work at?" he asked me and quickly resumed slurping at my toes.

"Seeing as I worked pretty hard to get to where I am I guess you could say that yeah, I'm pretty fond of what I do!" I replied sarcastically. "Gawd, you're a fucking foot freak man!! Fucking guy, sucking my toes like crazy through those smelly socks of mine!"

The sounds of slurping filled the room as he sucked my socked toes like mad. He held tightly to my calves as his tongue flicked over and over the bottoms of my feet. I hated to admit it but what he was doing to my feet had chills and thrills coursing through me like crazy. Linda had never gone after my feet except to tell me how funky they smelled when I would take my wingtips off when I was at her place after a long workday. I thought how had I been at her place that night instead of at home none of this would have been happening to me. After a while he stopped slurping at my toes and leaned down on the bed over my dick and balls. He glanced over at the digital clock on my night table and smiled from ear to ear.

"I would say that enough time has gone by Trevor," he said. "I think it's time to make you shoot a second load for me. Would you agree handsome guy?"

Before I could reply and say that it hadn't been a half-hour yet he spit liberally into his hand and gathered my pulsing dick into it.

"Ohhhhh," I panted as he squeezed my dick and began stroking it slowly. "H-here we go again and off I'm about to go again, JEEZ!!"

"Sure as shit you gorgeous fucking stud," Mike the burglar said menacingly. "We're going to be at this all fucking night. Come morning this dick of yours is going to be super-duper sore and your balls are going to be bone dry. I doubt your pretty girlfriend ever got you off half as many times as I'm going to make you cum!"

B-but it hasn't been a half-hour yet man!!" I finally grunted as he stroked me.

"Who gives a fuck?" he asked me. "A big strong guy like you can no doubt shoot more than a few loads within a short period of time. Man, I am going to milk you fucking parched you handsome stud."

As he spoke I shuddered miserably and my nipples came to life in the tit clamps, stinging and driving me crazy anew. He stroked me a little faster.

"Ohhhh you fucker," I grunted, burying my face in my pillow again. "Fuckin' raping me is what you're doing!"

"I haven't even gotten started on raping you handsome guy," he said and stroked me and stroked me and stroked me some more. "After you've shot this second load we'll see what other treasures and mementos you have around this place of yours."

"Ohhhhh man, just stop this and get out of here already man!!" I seethed as I felt myself getting close to shooting a second damned load onto my sheets.

He slurped at my stinking toes as he stroked my dick faster and faster. Chills and goose bumps broke out all over me. My nipples stung in agony.

"Oh God, yeah, yeah, getting me there again you miserable burglar!!" I seethed, lifting my head up off the pillow. "Ohhhhh yeah you son of a bitch, you got me creaming like a bitch in heat!!"

For the second time that night I spurted a good-sized mess of ball juice onto my bed sheets, grunting and groaning breathlessly as I came and came.

"Oh yeah, shoot that load for me you handsome fucking guy," the burglar said mockingly, continuing to stroke me more and more. "I love watching a big stud like you shoot his load. The look of ecstasy mixed with helplessness on that handsome face of yours drives me wild!"

He let my toes slip out of his mouth and when he had squeezed the last droplet of cum from me for that shot he let go of my dick. Again, it slapped hard against the sheets, landing in the new puddle of my jizz. I pressed my face into my pillow and screamed and roared in tortured agony as the tit clamps tortured the utter fuck out of my poor sensitive nipples anew.

"*Ohhhhhhhhhhhh!!!!!!!!*" I screamed muffled and pitifully into the pillow. "*Get these fucking things off my nipples man!! Please!!!*"

I heard him snickering meanly as he again climbed off the bed. When I looked up a few moments later I saw that he was standing over me. Tears of agony and rage had streaked my cheeks and I was sweating at that point. I felt my arms and legs starting to get numb and the smell of my more than day old socks was rancid.

"OH GOD, my poor nipples," I said softly up at him.

He smiled, reached down, and ran the tip of a finger

through the tears on my face. He put his tear soaked finger in his mouth and sucked it, a look of ecstasy on his face.

"Mmmmm, you sure do taste exquisite," he murmured. "And the way you talk so helplessly about your nipples really breaks my heart you handsome fuck..."

Then, he hunkered down at my night table and opened my underwear drawer.

"I always felt that there was something real kinky and erotic about going through a guy's underwear drawer," he said, reaching into the drawer and taking out a pair of my white briefs. "No object is more intimate than a guy's underpants. Not to mention that you can tell a lot about a guy from the kind of underpants he wears. Wouldn't you agree Trevor ol' boy?"

"I-if you say so man," I said miserably as he glanced in my underwear drawer.

"All white briefs Trevor, why is that?" he asked me. "You think you're a pure boy or something?"

"Nah, maybe I just find white briefs to be real comfortable," I replied sarcastically, not believing I was having this conversation.

He reached into his pocket and brought out the long knife he had used to get the drop on me earlier. I gulped loudly as I watched him slit a pair of my briefs at the crotch.

"Geez Trevor, it's a good thing you're not wearing these at the moment," he said with an insane looking grin on his face.

He slit the briefs in half and dropped them on the floor with my other ripped up pair that he had cut off me. I balled my bound hands into fists as he took a second pair of briefs from my drawer and slit them in half also.

"Wh-why are you doing this?" I asked him through trembling lips.

"Scared Trevor?" he asked me with a grin.

He put the knife back in his pocket and stood up. He helped himself to my gold chains and bracelets that were on my night table and my wallet. From my dresser top he took my Movado watch, the watch that Linda had given me recently.

I didn't make mention of that though. The way he had ripped up my briefs with that knife had been enough for me to realize that this guy was a little over the edge where sanity was concerned. I watched as he put my belongings into his backpack, except for my wallet. He opened the wallet and looked at the pictures I had in it. There was a picture of Linda and I, a picture of my brother's son, (who just happens to be my godson) and a picture of my parents. As I lay there totally trapped and helpless I wondered if I would ever see any of them again. Mike the burglar counted the hundred and fifty dollars cash that was in there and finally dropped my wallet into his backpack. My dick was fear-hard under me again and I again wondered miserably what that was all about. I wasn't feeling good about any of this, so why the fuck was my dick hard? Mike walked back over to me and stood at the side of the bed looking down at me. "Feeling good Trevor ol' boy?" he asked me and ran a hand over my raised feet.

"Yeah, just fucking great," I replied. "I've always wanted to be trapped in my own apartment by a nut like you!!"

"I would watch my mouth if I were you Trevor ol' handsome guy," he said to me. "You're really in no position to be cocky."

"S-sorry," I said despondently. "Fucked up position for a guy to find himself in though."

Mike sat back down on the side of my bed and again propped his booted feet up next to me.

"Lick," he said meanly.

I moved my head toward his feet and the clamps on my nipples pulled hard on my poor nubs.

"Owwwwww!!!" I gasped and pressed my mouth against one of his boots.

I licked it liberally at the tip and ran my tongue all over the side of it. He looked at me with total satisfaction showing in his eyes.

"Now, I want to hear about the best sex you ever had with one or more of your buddies while you were in the Air Force," he said to me and I stopped licking his boot and looked at him quizzically.

"Wh-what?" I asked him in shock.

"And don't lie and tell me that you never fooled around with any of your buddies in the service," Mike the burglar said meanly. "All you military guys are closet faggots!! Lick!!"

I again licked his boot and trembled miserably in the bondage.

"When you're done licking that boot you'll tell me all about it Trevor," he said commandingly. "And then I'm going to stroke a third load out of you."

My head spun miserably. I had never in my life talked about that day on the private beach when I had been with Ricky and David, two of my best buddies in the Air Force. And now this bastard was going to force that story out of me...

When Mike the burglar was satisfied that I had licked his boot enough, he pulled it away from my mouth and placed his feet on the floor. He leaned forward, looking at me menacingly, and ordered me to tell him about a sexual experience I'd had with my buddies while in the Air Force.

"O-okay, but you have to understand, we hadn't seen a woman in more than a few months," I began in explanation. "Just because this happened doesn't make me gay! And just because you're forcing me to shoot my load over and over doesn't fucking make me queer either man!!"

A look of aggravation came over Mike's face. He reached forward, grabbed my mustache, and tugged a few strands of hair out of it.

"Yowwwwwwwwwwww!!!!" I roared in agony into my pillow, muffling my screams of pain. "Oh FUCK, FUCK, that smarts you bastard!"

"Just tell me Trevor ol' boy," Mike said sternly. "Whether you're a faggot or not is of no consequence here. I know that all you military fucks are closet cases."

I lifted my head, pursed my lips miserably, and began.

"I had been in the Air Force for a little more than a year when this happened," I said in beginning. "Ricky's parents owned a private beach-house in Los Angeles that they used when the winters in New York became too cold for them. I guess you could say they had money, lots of money. Well, Ricky, David, and I had all been granted a week's leave of vacation time. The three of us decided to spend it in Los Angeles and Ricky's parents had been kind enough to let us use the beach house. It had two big bedrooms and plenty of space for the three of us to stretch out and have some real relaxation time. Ricky and David doubled up in one of the bedrooms and I took the other one by myself. We spent our first day in Los Angeles on Rodeo Drive the three of us decked out in our dark blue Air Force uniforms. Man, were the girls checking us out let me tell you. I figured that before the week was over I was going to land me some real good pussy no pun intended. On our second day there we decided to stay at the beach-house and just relax. The three of us were sitting around the living room in our sweats and tee shirts when Ricky suggested a swim in the ocean. David, a stocky but muscular buzz-cut blond guy said that sounded great to him and got to his feet as he said he would get his bathing suit. Ricky, a tall hand-some fucker with brown hair and dark eyes asked me if I wanted to join them as well as he pulled off his tee shirt, revealing a mus-cular rippled torso, shaming my muscular body. I told him that I hadn't thought to bring a pair of swimming trunks but for him and David to go on ahead and have fun, indicating that I would remain there and watch television. With a shit eating grin on his face Ricky told me to swim in my under shorts, indicating that it was a private stretch of beach and that there was no one around for miles to see us if I did so. I asked him if he was sure and he said he was positive, adding that one time he even swam naked out there."

"And nothing happened to you?" I asked him.

"Well, except for the fishes sucking my dick like crazy nothing happened," he said and we both laughed.

"I can see what your buddy Rick had in mind already," Mike the burglar said. "Go on."

I licked my lips and continued the story of the day at the

beach.

"The three of us walked out of the house, Ricky wearing a black Speedo brand bikini, David in a pair of black Speedo trunks that clung to his body, and I in my white BVD briefs.

Admittedly I felt rather strange and on display walking on a beach in my BVD briefs. Each of my buddies was wearing beach tong shoes and I was barefoot. I hadn't even thought to pack a pair of beach tongs and the sand was hot beneath my bare feet."

"Great fucking day for a dip in the waves huh guys?" Ricky asked us as we walked slowly across the beach.

"Yeah, you said it buddy," David said.

"I agreed as well but told them that we needed to get down to the water fast, as the sand beneath my naked feet was searing hot," I went on telling the burglar my tale. "Ricky said that that was no problem, that there was no need for my tootsies to be seared by the hot sand. That was what he called them, my tootsies. That said, Ricky scurried under my legs and before I realized it he had me hoisted and balanced perfectly atop his big broad shoulders. I chortled wildly, telling him what a strong fucker he was for sure. Ricky said that he hadn't worked his ass off like crazy during basic training for nothing. As he carried me nearly effortlessly he hooked his huge hands over the tops of my thighs to keep me well balanced atop his shoulders. David jokingly asked me how the air was up where I was perched and jokingly gave me a good-buddies slap on my BVDed ass. I told him it was just great, feeling like a king of sorts as I rode atop Ricky's huge shoulders. I figured what the fuck, telling them that at least my feet weren't suffering the intense heat of the sand anymore. Ricky laughed and yelled out "Yer toot toot tootsies buddy!"

I looked at Mike the burglar and saw that he was grinning from ear to ear.

"What's so funny?" I asked him.

"Shit man, you were beyond naïve," he said meanly. "Your two buddies had the fucking hots for you. You have no idea just how fucking hot you are do you?"

I pursed my lips in anger again.

"Tell me you didn't have a hard-on while your buddy was carrying you across that beach," he said demandingly.

"Strange as I felt about it, yeah, I did lay a major-sized boner-erection while I was up there on Ricky's shoulders," I said, continuing the story. "If Ricky felt it against his neck as he carried me he made no mention of it whatsoever. I of course wondered fleetingly what that was all about, but just attributed it to the lack of female contact lately. I just figured I would remedy that situation very soon in the evening, but little did I know at that moment that my two buddies would help me to alleviate that problem. When we got down to the wet sand my two buddies kicked their tongs off their feet and with me still atop Ricky's shoulders they walked into the cold ocean water. Ricky shivered and said that the water was real cold when he was thigh-high in it. The bastard jostled me jokingly on his shoulders and then let go of my thighs. I plunged bodily into the cold water in my BVD briefs."

As I relayed my story my dick was betraying me by getting harder and harder under my now aching hog-tied body. Just like I had to wonder at why I had gotten an erection when Ricky had carried me on his shoulders across that beach I had to REALLY fucking wonder as to the why of my erection while being held prisoner in my own damned apartment.

"I yelled at Ricky that the water was freezing and playfully splashed him while we all swam out further into the crystal clear water," I reluctantly continued, not really wanting the goddamned burglar to know what had transpired on that fateful day, me thinking how it would somehow really give him ammunition to use on me. "I swam out ahead of my two Air Force buddies and the cold water had caused my dick to become even harder and more plumped up in my BVDs. It pounded and pulsed like a thing alive in my briefs as I swam around. Ricky commented to David how the water temperature felt really good once you got used to it. David agreed with him wholeheartedly and then he asked me how I was feeling."

I licked my lips a few times before continuing…

"I told David that I was feeling real good and invigorated as he and Ricky swam over to me," I said, looking helplessly at the man who had me trapped in my damned apartment, a knowing look of what was coming next etched on his mean looking face. "Then, my two buddies each took a breath, held it, and disappeared under the water. Laughing, I asked them what they were up to now, but I didn't have to wait long for an answer because I felt their fingers grabbing at my briefs. They pulled my BVDs down under the water. I remember saying something stupid like, "Hey, what are you two jokers up to?"

Mike the burglar chuckled and propped his booted feet back up on my bed. He said the word "Lick" and I did as he said before continuing again with my blasted tirade.

"When my two buddies surfaced I was naked and it was Ricky who had my sopping wet BVD briefs all balled up in hand," I said and my dick pounded under me. "He chuckled meanly and said that he was real sorry but that we needed something that we could use as a ball. The jokester tossed my balled up briefs over my head to David who caught them. I really wasn't amused by all this and I demanded that they give me back my damned under shorts. I mean, I was feeling real vulnerable at that moment and my damned cock had betrayed me by getting hard in the cold water. I honestly did not think what they had done was funny at all. But David quipped that he thought it was hilarious and flung my stolen BVDs back over to Ricky who caught them. This game went on for a little while, my two buddies tossing my briefs back and forth over my head, out of my reach, preventing me from getting them back. But then, Ricky disappeared under the water, taking my briefs with him."

Mike the burglar snickered, knowing well what I was about to tell him next...

"I was bobbing there in the water with David, about to resume swimming even without my briefs on when I suddenly felt Ricky's lips close around my dick from behind me under the water," I said to the damned burglar, continuing my story. "I let out a gasp and froze in that spot, bobbing there. David asked me what was the matter. With a mocking look on his face he swam in real close to me. There was no doubt in my mind that David knew what the fuck was happening to me at that moment. As I floated there I blubbered and gasped that Ricky had my damned dick in his mouth under the water, stuttering in between speaking. My legs were spread wide under the water and I again told David in disbelief that Ricky was sucking my manhood down there. David chuckled and told me to relax. I nearly blanched when he gave my erect and cold nipples a squeeze and twist each. I gasped about them not being gay as chills coursed through my muscular body in the water. Well, maybe they were gay after all, but I wasn't, and I told them that, adding somewhat reluctantly that what Ricky was doing to me did feel great at that. David told me to just enjoy it and he squeezed and twisted my nipples again. Holding my damned tits in his fingers he said to pretend that it was a beautiful woman down there sucking my big meat. When Ricky couldn't hold his breath any longer he let my dick slip out of his mouth, leaving me hard and bothered down there. He swam to the surface and grinned at me from ear to ear. He barked the word "Gotcha" at me and tossed me my briefs.

I caught my briefs in my trembling hands as David ducked under the water next. Under the water David gobbled my big pulsing dick into his mouth next, running his hands over my long muscular legs at the same time. I groaned at Ricky that now David was sucking on me down there. Ricky swam around me, circling me like a shark. I sarcastically said how it was very obvious how they had planned all this. Ricky didn't deny it and followed up by asking if I had a problem with two good buddies getting me off. It felt too fucking good to make them stop, it really did man. The way David was sucking me under the water was like magic. I was able to feel my cum filled balls swinging in the waves. When David could no longer hold his breath he let my dick slip out of his mouth and surfaced. As he caught his breath he suggested that they do me together. The two men laid me in a prone position on the water, floating me there with my big hard pulsing dick sticking up for their pleasure and mine. What a sight that was let me tell you..."

At that point I could not wait for the damned burglar to stroke a third jizz shot out of me. Recounting this story for his perverted pleasures was driving me wild. I wondered what it was doing for him.

"So, as I floated there in the water on my back my two buddies bobbed at my sides, taking turns sucking my hard dick," I said. "They fed it to each other, stroking it as they sucked it too. My big balls were pulsing and hanging low in the cold water, a treat for any fish that happened by. None did though. As they sucked me and sucked me they said that whoever had me in their mouth when I came would be the one to carry me back across the hot sand atop their shoulders. Well, because it felt so fucking good what they were doing to me I held back for as long as I possibly could. But then, when I had been sucked to the point where I could not hold back even if I really wanted to I shot a good-sized hefty load of ball juice into Ricky's mouth. The greedy cock sucker swallowed every drop of me as David squeezed my nipples hard, twisting them, making me grunt and groan even louder as Ricky swallowed my ball juice."

"Shit man, those two guys really knew how to get you off good you handsome stud," Mike the burglar said breathlessly.

"I'm not done yet, there's more," I said, sounding annoyed. "When Ricky was done guzzling my jizz we all swam toward shore. I was feeling pretty good being that I had just had one of the most intense orgasms of my life. When we got close to shore Ricky hoisted me up to his shoulders and walked over to the spot where their beach tongs were. My two buddies slipped their tongs onto their feet and Ricky lowered me to the cool sand where they were standing. I jokingly told him that he had to lug me across the hot sand on his shoulders, being that he was the one who had been lucky enough to scoff down my ball juice. Looking at me intently he told me that they weren't done with me yet. As I stood there in the cool sand by the water Ricky squatted behind me, pushed my ass cheeks apart and plunged his tongue into my hole. Needless to say that I gasped loudly as chills went through me like crazy. David hunkered down in front of me and gobbled my semi hard dick into his mouth. My two buddies ran their hands up and down my long legs as they squatted there licking my hole and sucking my dick. I crossed my arms behind my head and curled my toes back in the wet sand as they brought me to heights of ecstasy that I had never known before."

"Shit man, you lucky fucking bastard," the burglar said, pushing one of his booted feet close to my face.

I gave his boot a fast lick before continuing with my story.

"They ate my hole and sucked my dick like crazy, working me into a frenzy until I was ready to shoot a second load for them," I said to the burglar. "I grunted like a marine as I stood there sweating in the sand as my two buddies feasted on me. I told them how I really got the feeling that they had planned all of this. I mean, lets face it okay? This wasn't something that straight guys like us did on the spur of the moment. After that there was no more talk from me as I shot a second load of creamy ball juice and David scoffed it down like he had never eaten before.

Mike placed his other booted foot near my face and I gave that boot a quick lick as well before concluding my story.

"When I was done shooting that second load I felt well spent," I said to him. "I stood there sweating as my two buddies got to their feet at my sides. We all smiled at each other. An ocean wave rolled in, bringing my white briefs with it. I picked up my briefs and told my buddies that it looked like I really hadn't needed them after all. We all chuckled at my remark. Then, Ricky hoisted me back onto his shoulders and carried me back into the water, followed by David. Needless to say man, those two fucking guys sucked me off a few more times out there in the water before we called it a day."

My story was done. Mike the burglar was looking at me intently, feverishly. Without a word he climbed onto the bed behind me, spit liberally into his hand, and grabbed my pulsing hard dick. He began stroking me slowly toward a third orgasm.

"Ohhhhhh man, just like my two Air Force buddies you sure do like making me shoot those loads for you," I grunted.

"Yeah, but unlike your two buddies I'm going to milk you till you can't fucking stand it handsome guy," he said meanly and stroked me faster. "I'm going to have you crazy with it by the time the sun comes up in the morning. And then we're going to go for more and more."

As the fucking guy stroked me a third time I thought about that day on the beach. Thinking about that caused me to get even harder in the burglar's grip. Thinking of him milking me repeatedly sent shivers of fear through me. I mean, there was just so much a guy could be made to cum after all. But then, my thoughts were cut short as I felt myself getting ready to shoot a third load. "Ohhh man, you fucking bastard," I seethed. "Getting me there already!!"

He slurped at my socked toes and then I came, shooting a third, but smaller load onto my bed sheets.

"Ohhhhhh yeahhhh yeahhh, you fucking bastard," I heaved breathlessly as he pulled hard on my dick, once again forcing every possible drop of sperm from me.

When I was done he again let go of my dick and it flopped down into the newest puddle of my jizz. My sensitive nipples stung and burned anew and I again screamed muffled into the pillow. At that point I realized just how miserable and numb my arms and legs were getting. I had been trussed up in that hog-tie for more than an hour at that point. Not to mention the fact that my dick was starting to feel sore and that I was sweating a bit uncomfortably... But alas, it would be quite a while before I was untied. Mike the burglar climbed off my bed and headed for my clothes closet. What now I wondered miserably...

He opened my sliding door closet and took out one of my suits. "Nice," he said, running his hand over the suit jacket still on its hanger. "Expensive suit handsome guy. You must really be a big deal where you work."

I watched helplessly as he took his knife out of his pocket and began slitting my blue pinstriped Armani suit down the back. I gulped as I thought of that blasted knife being dragged down my back. When my suit jacket was torn down the back he tossed the jacket to the floor and took the suit pants in his hands, holding his knife clenched in his teeth. He tore the suit pants down the center, a look of menacing insanity on his face. He tossed the remnants of my suit pants to the floor and took my charcoal colored Armani suit from the closet. He ripped that one up with his knife also before tossing it mindlessly to the floor with the other one.

"Wh-why are you doing this man?" I asked him as my dick grew fear hard under me and twitched in the puddle of my now cool jizz.

In response he simply smiled meanly at me and turned his back on me. I watched as he pushed my suits, my slacks, my sports jackets, my jeans, and dress shirts aside till he found what he was looking for. A look of despair filled my face as he held up my navy blue air force uniform, complete with light blue dress shirt and dark blue tie.

"Oh no, no man, please, please don't rip up my uniform!" I said pleadingly. "Shit man, that uniform means a lot to me!"

He seemed to think it over, his knife in one hand my uniform in the other.

"Tell you what Trevor ol' boy, I'll spare your uniform and you, as long as you do as I tell you while I'm here!" he said to me.

"Wh-what do you want?" I asked him.

Laughing, he tossed my uniform on the end of my bed and climbed on the bed behind me.

"I want you to get dressed Trevor," he said, placing the tip of the knife against the bottom of my socked foot.

I gulped again and clenched my teeth as he ran the tip of the knife against the bottom of my foot. What kind of sick pervert was this who had invaded my home I asked myself despondently and miserably, looking at the torn tatters of my slashed suits on the floor.

A little while later I was standing next to Mike the burglar in my bedroom. I had donned my air force uniform, complete with my lace-up patent leather shoes. Mike stood close by with the knife in his hand after having untied me from the bed. I was too weak and felt totally powerless to try anything as I stood there getting dressed. Surprisingly the uniform fit me rather well, mostly because I had kept myself in pretty good shape since my Air Force days. After I was fully clad in my Air force uniform the slimy fuck roped my hands behind me and pulled my dick and balls out of the fly opening in my uniform pants. I stood rigidly and practically at attention with my hands roped behind me and my dick and balls sticking out of the fly opening of my uniform pants as Mike the burglar stood in front of me, his knife pressed against the spot just under one of my earlobes. I was glad to be out of that damned hog-tie and also glad to have those torturous tit clamps off my nipples. However, I was not glad that Mike the burglar was still there and keeping me prisoner in my own apartment. Little did I know at that moment just how much time he and I were going to be spending together in my apartment that night.

"Damn, but you are beyond handsome," he murmured in a throaty sounding tone of voice as he caressed me with the tip of the knife.

"Pl-please man," I choked as he moved the knife over my cheek.

"Tell me Trevor Stevens, where do you keep the liquor?" he asked me and chuckled fiendishly.

Then, a few minutes later we were seated next to each other in the kitchen at my table. I was securely roped to my chair, my dick fear hard and pounding between my legs as my balls rested on the chair seat. My legs were spread apart and roped off at my ankles to the chair legs. A couple of bottles of scotch were on the table along with a tall glass with a straw in it. I had already been made to sip down two glasses of the scotch through the straw and I was feeling pretty tipped and buzzed as the burglar stroked me toward a fourth orgasm. Holding my pulsing dick in his hand he stroked me slowly, fast, and slowly again.

"Ohhh God, ha-has it been a ha-half hour already?" I asked him drunkenly, looking down and watching as he stroked me and stroked me.

"Heh heh, feeling good now eh handsome guy?" he asked me mockingly and gave my chest a good hard pat. "Tell you man, a few more glasses of that scotch there and I won't need to keep you roped up anymore."

"F-fucker..." I panted stupidly and felt myself getting close to shooting that fourth load. *"Ohhhhh, ge-getting there now you bastard...oh fucking fucks, it's like you've taken control of my damned jazzing cock"*

Mike's saliva slicked hand worked magic on my pulsing big dick. I shot a good-sized load of ball juice onto the floor under my table.

"Ohhhh shit, yeahhh..." I ranted, curling my toes back in my shoes and my head spinning as the burglar squeezed that fourth load out of me.

He held tightly to my dick and forced every possible drop out of me.

"Ohhhhh..." I panted as he rubbed the tip of his thumb against the slimy head of my dick, teasing my dick hole with the tip of another finger.

I sat there sweating in my uniform. He let go of my dick and I watched in tortured and drunkenly agony as he filled the glass again with the scotch.

"Oh no, no, no more man, please," I squeaked as he held the straw to my trembling lips.

With no choice other than to do as I was told I began sipping the scotch slowly through the straw. It burned on the way down and my head spun away even more. Fucking burglar was making me drunker than a marine on a weekend pass in the city. Through blurred vision I saw Mike smiling wickedly at me from ear to ear.

"Oh yeah, you military guys sure can scoff down the booze, that is for sure," Mike chortled meanly.

When the glass was empty, my head rolled back and the room was spinning.

"Ohhhhh shit man," I gurgled.

"Ready for some more fun Trevor ol' boy?" Mike asked me, reaching toward me, and tugging on my necktie.

"D-depends," I said incoherently. *"Wh-what the f-fuck do you have in mind for me now?"*

I lowered my head and watched as the burglar stood up.

"Wh-where are you going?" I slurred as he left the kitchen and walked into my living room.

He returned a few moments later with a very thin plastic stirrer in his hand.

"G-going to m-mix me a cocktail now?" I asked him stupidly.

"Oh no Trevor, not that," Mike the burglar said and pulled his chair close to mine.

He reached into his backpack, brought out a long white cloth, rolled it into a ball, and crammed the thing deep and far into my mouth.

"MMMMffff???" I asked him drunkenly.

"You're going to need that gag for this handsome guy," Mike said, holding up the stirrer.

He took my flaccid dick in his hand, spit onto the tip of it, and he and I watched as he squeezed my dick a few times, getting me semi hard and making his saliva drip into my slit. I looked at him wonderingly.

"Yeah I know, it hasn't been a half hour yet," he said. "But this time I'm not planning to milk you, at least not just yet."

Then, I watched in total and drunken horror as the burglar moved the tip of the thin plastic stirrer toward my dick slit.

"MMMffff!!!!" I screamed behind the gag, nodding my head desperately from side to side. "MMMffff…"

Slowly, he began inserting the stirrer into my slit, the pain like nothing I had ever felt before.

"RRRRRmmmfff!!!!" I sputtered as stinking sweat broke out all over me.

I was drunk, but not so far gone to reel in the pain the bastard was inflicting on me. I writhed miserably under the tight ropes, curled my toes back in my shoes, and cried big tears of agony as Mike inserted the stirrer further into my slit.

"Mmmmmmffff..." I wailed in total agony when he began thrusting the stirrer in and halfway out of my slit, fucking my slit like it was a pussy or something.

I again lolled my head back just so I didn't have to watch as my poor dick was tortured. But Mike grabbed a handful of my hair and yanked my head down, forcing me to watch.

"RRRRmmmfff!!!" I seethed at him.

Looking down at my poor dick tears fell from my eyes onto the stirrer in my slit. I shook, trembled, and cried like a fucking baby. Mike ran two fingers through my tears and licked them off, a look of sheer ecstasy on his face. Beads of piss formed around the stirrer as Mike pushed it even further into my poor dick. By now my dick was fear hard all over again and that damned stirrer was just about pushed to the halfway mark.

"Man, if this was war time and you were a fucking POW you would be telling the enemy anything they wanted to know," Mike said mockingly and again thrust the stirrer in and halfway out of my slit.

When the stirrer *was* more than halfway jammed into my slit Mike let go of my dick. My dick stood up long and hard with the stirrer sticking out of it, staring up at me, mocking me.

"Look at me you handsome fuck," Mike said meanly.

Slowly I looked up at him through drunken vision.

"Want that thing out of your piss hole?" Trevor ol' boy?" he asked me, tugging on my necktie.

With tears flowing uncontrollably from my eyes, I nodded my head up and down. I watched as he filled the tall glass with scotch again. I nodded my head miserably from side to side.

"Here's the deal handsome guy," Mike said, stirring the scotch with the straw. "I'll take the gag out of your mouth, you drink down every drop of this scotch, and then I'll take the stirrer out of your piss hole. After that I'm going to squeeze another load of Air force goop out of that magic dick of yours and then we're going to play another game."

I looked at him miserably, silently begging him to just get

the fuck out of my apartment. Glancing at the clock on the wall I was able to tell that it was now almost four AM. We had been at this shit for just about three hours at that point.

"You ready?" Mike asked me, his fingers on the gag.

I grudgingly nodded my head up and down. He slowly slipped the gag out of my mouth. Before feeding me the scotch he placed the side of the gag that had been in my mouth to his nose and mouth. He sniffed it heartily.

"Y-you s-sick fuck, get this th-thing out of my dick sl-sl-slit," I babbled incoherently.

Mike dropped the gag on the table and put the straw to my lips. With no choice whatsoever in the matter I sipped down yet another glass of scotch. When the glass was half empty Mike took mercy on me and allowed me to stop drinking. He placed the glass on the table and slowly pulled the stirrer out of my slit.

"Ayyyyyrr," I whimpered as the thing came painfully out of my slit.

When it was out Mike held my dick tightly in his hand and began stroking me.

"Ohhhh shit," I muttered, feeling like I had to piss and cum all at once. "SHIT, SHIT, SHIT…"

And that was just what I did. When I got to the point of climax, Mike held my dick aimed at the floor and I shot small spurts of cum. When I was done with that and breathless, I pissed long and hard on the floor under my table. Mike laughed meanly and hysterically.

"Shit, you military guys sure as fuck can drink, but you sure as fuck can't hold onto your liquor," Mike chortled.

"Wh-wha do you expect man?" I asked him angrily in my drunken stupor. "Y-you made me dri-drink almost a whole fucking bottle of scotch!"

I finished pissing and then Mike took my chin in his thumb and fingers and turned me toward him. We looked in each other's eyes and then he leaned in close to me. He pressed his lips against my trembling ones and kissed me passionately. I was shocked at the fact that I found myself responding to his kiss, forcing my tongue into his mouth and sucking hard at his lips.

"Godalmighty," Mike murmured when he stopped kissing me. "What a fucking night this turned out to be huh? And it's not even halfway over yet."

A few minutes later Mike told me we were going to play a game called "Find the Burglar." When I asked him how that was played he snickered meanly, plopped my Air force cap atop my head, and tied a black silk cloth over my eyes, blindfolding me. Then, I found myself out of the chair and standing on my now untied feet with my hands still roped behind me. My dick and balls were still hanging out of my uniform pants and Mike was holding me balanced by my upper arm. I tottered stupidly on my feet and pissed again onto the floor. The kitchen smelled of a rancid mixture of sweat, scotch, and piss.

"Okay Trevor ol' boy, you ready to play find the burglar?" he asked me.

"I-I don't know how," I slurred in reply.

"It's real easy," he said and squeezed my arm tight. "All you have to do is walk around your apartment here, blindfolded, of course, and try to find me. When you do find me I'll let you suck my dick."

"Aw no man, y-you're going to make me *suck your dick?*" I asked him drunkenly.

"I've gotten you off now what was it, five times?" Mike asked me, letting go of my arm and giving my flaccid dick a tug and a twirl. "So I think it's only fitting that you take your turn in getting me off eh handsome guy?"

Mike snickered as I grimaced miserably behind my blindfold. Then, holding me by my upper arms, he spun me around and around in place a few times in a clockwise direction.

"Uhhhhhnnnfff, get-getting dizzy," I slurred.

"Yeah, makes it all the more difficult for you to find me," Mike laughed.

When he let go of me and told me to start searching for him it took me a few good seconds to get myself balanced. I tottered and stumbled around my kitchen stupidly, bumping into things and even pissing on the floor again. Fucking mortifying to say the least. Fucker had really filled me up with scotch. As I stumbled blindfolded around my kitchen, Mike had gone into my living room with his big backpack. He helped himself to a lot of my compact discs, my videotapes, and even the small collection of DVDs that I had started.

"Man, I sure wish I could get that big state of the art television out of here," I heard Mike say as I made my way blindly toward the living room. "But I sure as hell will settle for the VCR and DVD players."

I was able to hear my VCR and DVD players being packed into his big knapsack.

"Best haul I ever made," Mike said as I came stumbling into the living room. "And what a bonus to go with it."

"O-okay f-fucker, I know you're here somewhere," I gurgled miserably. *"I-I can fuc-fucking shm-smell you."*

"Heh heh," Mike snickered. "Man, even with that blindfold covering those pretty eyes of yours you are too fucking beautiful Trevor ol' boy."

"Yeah, you're in here," I said and pulled madly at the ropes binding my wrists. "F-fucking burglar."

I heard Mike walk over to me and then he pulled my blindfold down, leaving it dangling around my neck.

"Y-yeah, *knew you were in here,"* I slurred stupidly.

"Yeah, you found me Trevor ol' boy," Mike said and pulled down the zipper on his jeans.

He pressed his lips against mine and kissed me and kissed me as he took his giant dick and big balls out of the fly opening of his jeans. I again forced my tongue into his mouth and sucked at his lips before we stopped kissing.

"Okay, get down there and suck my dick you gorgeous fuck," Mike commanded, toying with the knot in my necktie.

I looked at him through my blurred vision and slowly slid to my knees in front of him. I sniffed his dick and balls a few times. They smelled of sweat and a little piss thrown in. Then, I wrapped my lips around the burglar's semi hard dick and began sucking.

"Ohhh yeah, yeah you fucking gorgeous bastard," Mike crooned.

He took my Air force hat off my head, tossed it onto the couch, and ran his fingers through my hair as I sucked and sucked his dick. In between sucks I lapped at his big hairy balls, tongue bathing them real nice for him.

"Ohhh yeah, fucking hot Air force boy I got here," Mike muttered throatily and slipped his big fat dick back into my mouth.

I ran my tongue all over it, poked the tip of my tongue into his slit, and sucked him some more. All the while I was sucking him I saw myself on the beach that day with my two Air force buddies Ricky and David as they took turns sucking my dick. Even after I had been carried back over the hot sand, my two buddies settled me into a chair and knelt before me, still taking turns sucking my dick. Kneeling before me as I was now kneeling before the man who had invaded my home. As I thought of Ricky and David and as I sucked the burglar's dick, my dick grew hard between my legs all over again.

"Ohhhh man, I'm getting close you handsome fuck!" Mike swore meanly and forced his dick deep into my throat. "Ohhhhrrr yeah, fucking hot Air force fly boy I got here."

"GGGrrrrmmmfff," I sputtered and could not breathe as the burglar fucked my throat like crazy.

My head spun and spun and then I felt his hot juices flood my throat.

"RRRRmmmfff..." I gasped as I was fed Mike's juices.

"Oh yeah, swallow me you handsome stud, drink my fucking ball juice!!" Mike ranted, thrusting in and out of my throat as he seemed to cum and cum in a never-ending gusher. "Oh yeah, see the effect you have on me handsome guy."

When he was done he let his dick slip out of my mouth and I knelt there with my head hanging down, not feeling all that great, with my dick and balls still sticking out of my uniform pants.

"Pl-please let me go man," I whispered, my head hanging

just over his black work boots.

When Mike moved his foot closer to me I leaned down further and gave his boots a few licks and kisses each. I looked up at him and saw that he was smiling with total satisfaction.

"Shit man, even though I just got off I can't let you go yet man," he said, sounding as if he actually felt sorry for me. "I'm just getting myself started on you fly boy."

A look of total dismay clouded my face as he reached down and yanked me to my feet by a handful of my hair.

"Ayyyyrrr..." I seethed as he pulled me to my feet. "Fucker."

Back in the kitchen, Mike got my uniform pants off me over my black patent leather lace-up shoes and my blue socks. Leaving the top portion of my uniform on me and my hands tightly roped behind me he slumped me over my kitchen table with my legs dangling off the end and spread wide, exposing my pink ass hole. A feeling of utter terror consumed me as he roped my ankles to the table legs, keeping my legs pulled apart and my hole visible.

"Wh-wha-what is this?" I gasped, still in a drunken stupor.

"Ah, you'll find out soon enough handsome guy," Mike said and reached between my legs and grabbed my dangling dick.

"Arrrhhhhh shit," I grunted as he began stroking my now sore dick, not even bothering to lubricate it this time around. "Ohhhh FUCK, goin' to force another damned load out of me huh you pervert?"

It took a while this time but eventually I popped a small load.

"Ohhhh yeah, you fucker, driving me batty," I panted as I felt a small spurt of cum erupt from my dick.

It hurt slightly as I came due to having that damned stirrer in my slit earlier. I shook and trembled atop the table as Mike let go of my dick and sauntered over to my kitchen utensil drawer.

"You know Trevor, that is a great looking piece of ass you got there," Mike said and opened the utensil drawer. "That pretty girlfriend of yours ever tell you that?"

"Y-yeah, er, no, shit, I can't think straight," I stammered stupidly. "Fucking got me all drunk and stupid."

"No matter," Mike chuckled and took a wide long handled spatula out of the utensil drawer. "A good spanking should jar that memory of yours."

"Oh no, no," I whispered in despair.

Mike rubbed the spatula over my round globe shaped ass cheeks and gave them a few light taps with the spatula.

"Please man, don't do this to me," I pleaded.

Then, Mike gagged me again before really whaling into my butt cheeks with the spatula. He began by holding the flesh of one of my ass cheeks tightly in one hand while thrashing the other cheek repeatedly with the plastic kitchen spatula.

"RRRRRmmmmffff!!!!" I seethed more in anger than anything else at that point.

It wasn't bad enough that this faggot pervert had invaded my home, kidnapped me, robbed me, milked my dick repeatedly, got me drunk, tortured my cock with a liquor stirrer, made me stagger around my apartment blindfolded, made me suck his cock, but now he was fucking spanking me as if I had been a misbehaved child.

"RRRRRRmmmmffff!!!" I sputtered as he beat my ass cheek harder and harder with each blow.

He held my other ass cheek painfully tight in his hand and squeezed the fuck out of it as he rapped me and rapped me and rapped me with the damned spatula. When I had purchased that damn spatula at Lechter's I never once entertained thoughts of it being used this way. I thrashed wildly and drunkenly atop the table as the bastard went on and on rapping my ass cheek. Large tears slid from my eyes as I felt my poor ass cheek turning crimson. When he had delivered what felt like close to one hundred lashes with that spatula he still went on and on. My poor ass cheek felt like there were welts all over it. I am not ashamed to admit that he had me crying like a fucking little kid at that point.

"Oh man, what a great piece of ass you got back here

Trevor ol' boy," Mike snickered and spit a few times into my exposed bunghole.

"Mmmmfff???" I gasped and looked back at him.

He let go of my ass cheek and grabbed the one he had just spanked the fuck out of. He leaned down, gave my ass cheeks a kiss each and then began rapping the fuck out of the other one, just as hard as he had done with the first one.

"GGGrrrrmmmmfff!!!" I wailed madly and lay my head back down on the table in misery.

"It's a good thing I gagged you for this huh Trevor ol' boy?" he asked me. "The way I'm working these ass cheeks of yours over you would be screaming loud enough to wake the dead."

He held my crimson ass cheek tightly and meanly in his hand, squeezing it hard as he paddled my other cheek till it shone as red as the other one. A few times he spit into my hole. I shuddered to think what the hell he was priming me for back there. I lay there sweating, gasping, and grunting behind the gag crammed in my mouth as my poor ass cheeks were turned to mince meat.

"*RRRRmmmmffff!!!*" I cried out miserably.

Finally, after beating the hell out of both my ass cheeks a few times more each the bastard stopped, dropping the spatula on the floor. He ran his hands over my very wounded, very red ass cheeks. Over and over he spit into my hole. When I felt his fingers prodding my moist hole I nearly flew off that table, save for the fact that I was tightly tied to it.

"Oh yeah, I have to fuck you now Trevor ol' boy," Mike panted, reaching for the zipper on his jeans. *"I have to fuck you now!!"*

I lifted my head up and looked back at him, shaking my head frantically from side to side, tears streaming down my face.

"Don't worry handsome boy, I'll lube you even better," he said meanly, his big meat stick now sticking out of the fly opening of his jeans.

He reached around me and grabbed the full bottle of

scotch that was still on the table. He found a funnel in the utensil cabinet and I grimaced when he plunged the thin end of the funnel into my hole.

"This will have you feeling real good in no time Trevor ol' boy," Mike said, holding the bottle slightly tipped over the funnel opening. "This will have your head and the rest of you flying in no fucking time."

With my head craned back I watched in agony as he slowly poured the contents of the bottle through the funnel and into my hole. In less than a half-minute I felt my head spinning. I was more than drunk at that point; I was a fucking blasted flyboy. Mike poured a quarter of the bottle of scotch into my hole then took the funnel out.

"Oh yeah, nice slick tight looking hole handsome guy," Mike said and leaned down to rim some of the scotch off the walls of my hole.

"Mmmmmfffff!!!" I gasped, as his tongue seemed to work magic back there.

My ass cheeks seemed to twitch with a life of their own and my hole felt as if it were on fire.

"Oh man, *you want* me to fuck the tar out of you man," Mike said and then I felt the tip of his dick pressing against my virgin (not for long) hole.

Slowly, he slid his meat tool up inside me.

"RRRRRmmmfffff!!!" I wailed and writhed on the table.

Drunk and blasted as I was, it still felt awful as the burglar slid his dick further inside me. He spanked my poor ass cheeks hard as he slid all the way inside me. Why the fuck do guys who are fucking other guys always spank the ass of the guy they are fucking? He thrust his big dick in and out of my hole, driving me crazy with the pain. I'm sure that had I not been drunk it would have hurt a good deal more.

"Oh yeah you fucking hot guy, you're going to make me shoot a second load of spunk," Mike grunted and clutched one of my ass cheeks hard in his hand. "Oh yeah, goin' to spew my mess right into your hole no less you gorgeous fuck!!"

I was by then sweating like a pig, my hair hanging down in my face, and sweat dripping into my eyes from my hair and forehead. He held my hips, spanked my ass cheeks, and thrust in and out of me like a madman.

"Ohhhh yeah, getting there now you stud!" Mike grunted and then I felt his hot juices again, this time flooding my hole. "Arrrrr yeah!!! Cummin' like a damned bitch in heat!!"

As he spewed inside me, he rapped the sides of my thighs hard, pinched my ass cheeks, and thrust in and out, in and out, till he was spent. When he was done, his dick slipped out of my hole and he landed atop me on the table, hugging me tight.

"Oh yeah Trevor Stevens, fucking beautiful guy you are," he whispered in my ear and suckled my earlobe a few times.

He climbed off me, untied my ankles from the table, and in a quick move heaved me off the table to my feet by a handful of my hair.

"RRRMMMfff..." I roared behind my gag.

"Man, you are looking totally wasted Trevor ol' boy," Mike said meanly, pushed my head down and sent me flying against a wall, head first.

My head hit the wall hard and I was knocked into unconsciousness.

When I came to a little while later, Mike had me strewn across the tabletop in my kitchen, this time on my back with my feet dangling off the end of the table. The gag was out of my mouth, my hands were still tightly roped behind me, and my dangling feet were now tightly trussed at the ankles. My Air force issued black patent leather shoes were off my feet and my blue dress socks from the day before were really stinking like you would not believe at that point.

"Uhhhhhhnnn," I groaned miserably as I came to atop the table.

"Feeling okay handsome guy?" Mike asked me, looming menacingly over me. "Hope your head isn't hurting too badly. More than likely you're going to have a big bump there come tomorrow."

"Oh GAWD, oh God man, *y-you fucked me in the ass!!*" I ranted miserably, still feeling drunk and stupid. "Fuck, if I weren't all trussed up like this I would kill you man!!"

"Good thing I'm keeping you all trussed up like a caught chicken then eh fly boy?" Mike asked me and reached down to give my nipples a hard tweak.

"Accccccc!!! Shit!! Why couldn't you have treated this like the rest of the people and places you've robbed man?" I asked him, lifting my aching and spinning head up off the table. "Why did you have to kidnap me and do what you've done to me?"

"None of the others that I robbed were as ruggedly hand-some and delicious looking as you Trevor ol' guy," Mike respond-ed and leaned down over my semi hard and aching dick.

He gave my dick a few licks before slurping it greedily into his mouth.

"Ohhhh," I grunted and lay my head back down as he sucked me heartily, tugging on my balls at the same time.

"Ohhhh shit, goin' to make me shoot another damned load," I complained as my head spun faster and faster.

When my dick was hard, pulsing, and aching Mike took it in his hand and looked at me with a wicked grin on his face.

"Told you when I first captured you Trevor, that before I walk out of here I'm going to have you shooting dry loads," Mike said tauntingly to me. "It'll be days before you'll be able to have sex with that pretty little girlfriend of yours."

"J-just make me cum and get it over with man!!" I ranted in a high-pitched tone of voice as he held my hard dick in his hand. "Fuck man, my dick is aching!!"

Smiling, Mike gave my dick a few hard pulls and I came again, shooting a very small spurt of cum from my dick hole.

"Ayyyyyyy!!" I screeched. "C-can't believe how many times you've made me pop my load fucker!"

"Kind of has you falling in love with me eh Trevor?" Mike asked me, squeezing the last droplets of my small spurt from my dick. "Man handsome guy, by the time the sun rises you will be so milked that you won't believe it."

I looked up at my wall clock and saw that it was nearly five o'clock in the morning.

"H-how, how much longer do you plan to keep this shit up?" I asked as the burglar ran his tongue over my sweat soaked and stinking balls, trying to pretend that I had not heard his comment about the sun rising.

Mike lifted my head up off the table and force-fed me some more scotch.

"You're starting to sound slightly sober fly boy," Mike said as I drank the scotch. "Can't have that now can I?"

I simply looked at him miserably. When I was again good and stinking drunk, I watched as Mike again slurped my poor dick into his mouth. I nearly passed out as he sucked me and sucked me all over again. This time when I came, I did shoot a dry load. I felt an intense tingling in my dick but nothing came out of it. I found that could drive a guy crazy. I wanted to scream and rant madly at Mike as I felt his mouth engulfing my dick again, but sometime between making me drink more scotch and sucking my dick, he had gagged me again. After I shot yet another dry load, I watched as Mike knelt down at my dangling socked and tied feet. He sucked my toes a few times and licked my stinking feet all over for a while before gobbling my dick back into his mouth again.

By seven AM I was beyond wasted and tired. Mike had me off the table and standing propped against a wall in the kitchen. I stunk of sweat as he held me tightly by my arm, balancing me on my tied feet.

"Well Trevor Stevens, I've got what I came for plus a whole lot more," Mike said to me as I stood there with my head hanging down. "Sure as fuck wish that I could take you with me as well but you don't fit in my knapsack."

He laughed at his own stupid joke.

"So until we meet again I wish you a fond farewell," he said, grabbed a handful of my hair and knocked the back of my head hard against the wall.

"Uhhhhffff..." I gasped, slid to the floor, and fell again into unconsciousness.

When I came to it was eight AM, the sun was shining, and I felt like an eighteen-wheeler truck had run over me. I came to in my bed. As I sat up, I wondered if it could have possibly all been a bad dream. But when I saw the tatters of my underpants around my waist and that my blue socks were gone from my feet I knew that it had all been real. The fucker had carried me back to my bedroom and he did take my damned socks, along with everything else that he had stolen from me. I felt horribly hung over as I plodded to the bathroom on my bare feet. I knelt over the toilet and retched and retched. It was long overdue believe me. I found my Air force uniform on the floor of the kitchen. I was relieved that he hadn't taken that, or worse, destroyed it. My wallet, jewelry, CDs, DVDs, VCR, and DVD player were all gone though. All those things could be replaced I consoled myself. I called in sick to work and then called the police. Clad in shorts and a tee shirt after a long and hot shower I told the two cops about how I was robbed and assaulted by a burglar during the night. I told them that he had roughed me up, skipping over the parts where he had raped me. They made comment about the fact that I seemed to be slightly drunk. I explained how Mike the burglar had forced me to guzzle my own scotch. I gave them a description of him and they said they would do what they could about catching him and getting at least some of my stuff back. They told me that my report sounded a lot like the other people in the area who had been robbed while they were sleeping, except for the fact that I had been roughed up a bit. God almighty, if they only knew just how VERY roughed up I had been they would not have believed it. Or perhaps they would I reconsidered a short while later, they were cops after all. I thanked them and saw them to the door. When they were gone, I locked the door and shuffled to the bedroom to catch up on the sleep I had missed out on the night before. I (stupidly?) left my window wide open and the shade up...

The End

The Night before Graduation

A note from the author: Those of you who know me and those of you that have read my earlier books know that I have a severe fetish not only for men's black dress socks but for men's business attire as well. With this latest book I now bring to the surface, write about and eroticize my fetish for police uniforms. In my opinion nothing looks more commanding, strong and authoritative than a ruggedly handsome guy decked out in a police uniform. It feeds my business attire fetish as well seeing as the cop's uniform, like a business suit consists of black dress socks, a shirt and tie and highly shined black lace-up boots or perhaps knee high rubber boots (rubber boots being another fetish for many of us out there.) Besides the splendor and majestic look of a police officer's uniform I must say that I find myself to be equally entranced by the New York City police cadet's uniform, the rookie uniform if you would. The navy blue trousers with the stripe down the side, the tight fitting gray shirt and black thin tie all brought together with a pair of highly shined clonky looking lace-up shoes looks totally magnificent on these young fresh handsome, sometimes innocent looking rookies. With these police cadets in mind I give you the story "The Night before Graduation."

My name is Robert Brolin, Officer Robert Brolin to be exact. I'm a New York City Police Officer and damned proud of it let me tell you bud. What I want to tell you about happened back when I was still a police recruit, a rookie. What with all the Internet fantasies and erotic magazines out there nowadays detailing all those cop fantasies I figure that mine should spark some interest in a few people. And this was no fantasy bud, this was real, this happened and it happened to yours truly telling the tale. It was the night before my graduation from the New York City Police Academy. My friends had had a gathering at my best buddy John's house to celebrate my impending graduation the next day. Along with John, Howard, Dennis, and Rodd were also there to join in the celebration. We all met at John's house at eight PM. I arrived still dressed in my police rookie uniform, a dark blue jacket, dark blue pants with a dark blue silk stripe down the sides, a gray button down shirt with my nametag on it, a black cotton tie and black spit shined clonky police issued lace-up shoes. When I arrived at John's house, my buddies all patted me on the back, shook my hand, and presented me with a few (cold) six packs of beer.

"Hey guys, this is great!!" I said, shucking off my jacket and tossing it on the back of a chair. "Let's celebrate."

"Hell yeah," John said. "But this is just for tonight buddy. After graduation when you're a police officer, no beer drinking on the job."

At that comment, we all laughed but I admit I did take it seriously. I planned to be one of the best cops New York City had ever seen. We sat around the kitchen table, all of us sipping and gulping beers and just talking about general things.

"So Bobby, are you all ready for the big day tomorrow?" John asked me. "All ready to patrol a beat in scary New York City?"

I ran a hand through my dark straight hair and smiled.

"As ready as I'll ever be," I said, holding up my beer.

"To our good buddy," John said, holding up his beer. "May he always be safe as a police officer, may he never encounter anything really bad, and may he always be our friend."

We all clinked our beer cans together and took a long gulp each.

"Thanks John," I said, smiling.

"No problem bud," he said to me.

As John served me my second beer, I loosened my tie and leaned back in my chair.

"What time is the graduation ceremony tomorrow?" Howard asked me.

I took a gulp of my second beer and said "Twelve thirty in the afternoon."

"That's good," Howard said happily. "That way you won't have to rush home to bed tonight."

"Nope," I replied, holding up my second beer. "Plenty of time to enjoy the party."

I took a hearty gulp of my beer and John slid a third one over to me.

"Drink up buddy boy," John said. "It's your night."

My friends all smiled at each other as I gulped my beer. A half-hour later, I had drunk four and a half cans of beer. Looking around the table, I saw that my buddies had not even finished their first ones.

"I-I got to pee," I said, mimicking Forrest Gump.

My buddies all laughed hysterically and I could not help but join in. I was plastered, to say the least. My usual beer intake is two cans at the most. Here I had consumed nearly five and my buddies were there to make sure I celebrated even more.

"Here, finish this first," John said, putting his half-full can of beer to my lips.

As I chugged down what was left of John's beer I suddenly felt a hand undoing my tie.

"H-hey, whass goin' on?" I slurred after I had finished the beer.

"Relax Bobby," Howard said, putting his can of beer to my lips and making me drink it. "We're just making you a bit more comfortable and helping you celebrate."

I drank that beer also and the need to piss was starting to become overwhelming. My vision blurred and the room spun in front of me. My buddies helped me to my feet and then I felt the buttons of my shirt being unbuttoned.

"Wh-whass goin' on?" I asked again.

This time I received no reply and then I felt a hand on my trousers button and they unceremoniously slid to my ankles. Moments later, I found that all I was wearing was my white Jockey briefs, my thick navy blue calf length cotton socks, and my black spit polished clonky lace-up shoes. Fuck, but somehow those buddies of mine had managed to get me stripped lickety split let me tell you man.

"Hey, holy crap, looka me here, I'm outa uniform," I slurred stupidly. Those buddies of mine were then touching my very muscular and well-toned body everywhere, fuck, they were squeezing my tight ass cheeks through my briefs, and fuck of all fucks, they were stealing sucks and slurps on my big ol' nipples, and holy total fuck, they were squatting down to caress my strong tree trunk like legs, thighs and calves. I felt like I had become the goddamned meat market.

"H-hey guys, what is thisss?" I slurred. "I ain't no god-damned homo…"

"Just helping you to celebrate and have a really good time Bobby," John said directly into my ear and snapped the elastic in my briefs against my skin.

He sucked my earlobe into his mouth and ran his tongue over it a few times, brazenly sucking on it at the same time.

"Ohhhhhhhh God, wh-wha-what are you guys doin' to me here???" I asked.

"Okay guys, he's sloshed," John said jovially. "And ready."

Dennis and Howard each grabbed one of my legs as John and Rodd each grabbed my upper body. All together, they hoisted me off the floor, up, and over their heads.

"WHOA!!!! H-hey, p-put me down you guys," I said as they lugged me toward John's bedroom.

I fell into a semi state of unconsciousness. When I came out of it I found myself tied at the wrists and ankles in a spread eagle position to John's bed. My big whopper-sized cock was piss hard, solid as a board, aching for relief and raging in my briefs. I looked around in total shock and saw my four buddies standing around me. Fuck, they were all stripped naked and to add to that, their cocks were as hard as mine was in my briefs. I smiled at the sight of them and laughed hysterically.

"Hey guys, great fucking joke!" I said happily. "Now if you would, please untie me so that I can get to the bathroom. I have to fucking piss like you would not believe."

They all looked at each other and smiled meanly.

"I don't think so Bobby boy, at least not yet," John said, chuckling.

"Wh-what do you mean?" I asked nervously, my head still spinning from the all the beer I had consumed.

In response I watched as Dennis and Howard unlaced my size ten and a half shoes, slipped them slowly from my feet, sniffed the inside of each shoe, and then began licking one of my socked feet each, sniffing my rancid socks heartily in between licks.

"Ohhhhhh shit," I said in total shock. *"Wh-what the fuck are you guys doing?"*

I looked up at John in disbelief.

"Th-they're fucking licking and sniffing my stinking feet man!!" I sputtered drunkenly.

"And that's just the beginning," John said fiendishly. "Let's see how much control you have Officer."

"Wh-what do you mean?" I asked desperately.

"You have to hold that cock filled with piss till we're done with you," John said. "And that isn't going to be for quite a while."

"Holy fuck, and what if I do piss you bastard?" I asked him snidely.

"Well then, not only will you soak up your Jockey shorts but you'll also be punished with countless whacks to your hot ass with this," John replied, holding up a round leather paddle. "This is the same paddle that I whacked numerous pledges with when I was in college."

"Shit," I whispered as John and Rodd squatted at my big pink nipples.

They each slurped one of my nipples into their mouths and sucked them, hard.

"Fuckers," I said angrily. "Some friends all of you are! Goddamned guys, treating my man sized nipples like they were your girlfriend's tits or something!"

"Oh come on you love it," Dennis said, holding one of my bound-socked feet in his hands.

Dennis and Howard toyed with my smelly socks, rolling them up and down as they continued licking my feet and sniffing them. John and Rodd went on and on sucking my big nipples with real and total gusto. I could not get myself untied to save my life, struggle as I may, and my cock was hard as steel in my briefs. I grunted in a mixture of ecstasy and anger as I lay there being mauled and feasted upon.

A little while later the need to piss was *really* intense and I begged and pleaded with my buddies to untie me. They ignored me and went right on sucking my nipples and licking and sniffing my feet. I even went so far as to tell them that if they untied me and let me go to the bathroom that I would let them retie me to the bed and go on having their fun with me. Of course they more than likely didn't believe me. But that they ignored also, knowing that I was bullshitting.

"God you guys, please, *please,*" I pleaded.

John and Rodd abandoned my nipples and ran their tongues over my hairy chest and down to my stomach region, taking turns poking their tongues in my belly button and probing it, tickling me slightly.

"Uhhhffff!!!" I said as my six-foot muscular body squirmed on the bed.

They were really tickling me now by tonguing my belly button and I thought that for sure I would piss in my damned briefs, guaranteeing a hard paddling for me.

"Tomorrow when you graduate from the police academy you'll be thinking about this," John said, looking up at me as Rodd tongued my briefs now. "And I promise you'll get a rage hard boner in your cute uniform pants."

"You fucking bastards!!" I said, managing a smile, nearly cracking up in laughter as my belly button was lick/tickled.

Then, John and Rodd pulled my briefs down in the front and tucked them under my big juicy size of kiwi balls. My cock stood up long, straight, hard, fat, and pulsing. It was filled to overflowing with piss and filling up more every second. After all the beers I had drunk I wasn't surprised that I had to piss so badly.

"AW man, now you deranged mugs really got me on display here," I bantered, my head raised as I looked down at my steely erection and juicy balls.

"Shall we?" John asked Rodd, smiling across at him over my muscular body.

"Yes, let's," Rodd replied.

They each took one of my big balls into their mouths and began working them hard, tonguing the fuck out of them, sucking them, and applying pressure to them with their mouths.

"Oh gawd in his heavens!!!" I screamed and bucked wildly on the bed. "Ohhhh you fuckers, *fucking guys are eating my damned balls!!*"

Now I needed not only to piss, but I wanted to cum as well. Man oh man, my fucking meat stick was suffering to shoot a load like you would not fucking believe. I must have the most sensitive balls and nipples in the world because whenever they're even slightly touched I become totally fucking roused and boned. At the moment I was totally boned...I was harder than a fucking diamond bud... Dennis and Howard untied my feet, rolled my sopping wet saliva soaked socks off my big feet, and retied my now bare feet to the ends of the bed. They began licking my smelly bare feet and even sucked my rancid toes.

"Man, his feet really do fucking stink," Dennis commented.

Howard didn't reply, but only continued slurping on the toe

that he had in his mouth. When John and Rodd stopped working my balls they were swollen and pulsing like crazy.

"You're doing well Rookie boy," John said. "You really are holding onto that piss."

"B-but I won't be able to hold it much longer," I said desperately, sweating miserably now.

John and Rodd licked my smelly hairy armpits a little bit each as Dennis and Howard went on licking my bare feet.

"Wh-when will you guys be done?" I asked through clenched teeth, chills coursing through me.

A bead of piss appeared on my cock slit and slid down the shaft.

"Oh God no," I said in a high-pitched tone of voice.

I managed to hold it though, finding that I had pretty good control. But then my control was about to be tested even more. All four of my buddies abandoned the areas of my body that they were playfully abusing and each of them picked up a can of beer.

"Okay buddy boy, here we go," John said. "If you can down at least two of these cans of beer without pissing we'll untie you."

"O-okay," I said, not really believing that I would be able to hold it.

Rodd held my head up straight, John put the can to my lips, and I drank. Dennis and Howard resumed licking my bare feet. It seemed like they just couldn't get enough of my big old stinky feet. It was my feet that seemed to have been the prize they really sought I noticed. When I was done with the first can of beer my head was spinning and my cock was leaking beads of piss.

"H-hurry up and g-give me the other one," I said stupidly and drunkenly. "I-I can't hold on much more."

As I gulped down the second beer Dennis and Howard untied my feet. When my feet were freed I pulled them away from Dennis and Howard. Just as good as it felt having them lick my stinking feet I still wanted them to stop enjoying themselves so much at my expense. I finished the second beer and John and Rodd untied my wrists, keeping their promise. Once untied I bolted from the bed and ran out of the bedroom and to the bathroom like a bat outa hell and then, standing over the bowl in just my briefs I held my throbbing cock as steady as possible in my hand and pissed and pissed like crazy into the bowl. Drunk as I was I didn't lose my aim once; I pissed thick, frothy and perfectly into the bowl...

"Ohhhhh," I sighed loudly as relief filled me. *"Shit, you guys are too much!!! What a fucking celebration!!"*

I pissed for what seemed like forever, my frothy yellow brew sounding real sexy somehow to me as I dibbled it in the bowl, but then I was finally done. I dripped the last droplets of piss into the toilet and flushed. I was feeling totally plastered from all the beer that they had chugged into me. When I turned around John was standing there along with my other three buddies. They were looking at me hungrily.

"Wh-what now guys?" I asked, knowing all too well what they were up to.

All at once they grabbed me, lifted me up off the floor, and carried me back to the bedroom.

"Ohhh fuck, you guys, come on now, no more of this," I panted as they quickly retied me to the bed.

I was too smashed to do anything to stop them, and to be totally honest I don't think that I really wanted to stop them. They began forcing me to chug more beer, they again slobbered over and licked my feet, sucked hard at my nipples and balls, and continued the erotic abuse well into the night. It wasn't long before I had to piss again. After a good while they untied me from the bed, allowed me to use the bathroom, but once again trussed me back up for *still more* of what was being dished out on me. The night before my police academy graduation is a night I will never, ever forget. Thanks guys, the four of you are the best friends a guy could ever ask for.

The End

Officer Nevaready

It was exactly two months ago today when this happened... and it shouldn't have happened...shittiest thing in the world to do to a New York City cop if you ask me. My name is Edward Nevaready, Officer Edward Nevaready to be exact. I don't think a fucking day goes by that my cop buddies don't tease and razz me about my last name.

"Hey Eddie, are you ready? Nah, he's Never ready, right Nevaready?" my buddies would torment me in the locker room while we would be getting into our police uniforms before morning roll call.

"Hey Nevaready, how long does it take you to get ready?" was another good one they would heap on me, mostly while I would be bending to lace up my clonky police issued shoes.

And on and on it went all the jokes about the last name I was cursed with. And like a good cop who loved his buddies and police brothers I took it. I took it with a smile and the occasional "fuck you" as well, har, har har...

I'm six feet three inches tall; I have blond wavy hair, crystal blue eyes, and a totally lean and very muscular body from working out at the gym religiously. I'm twenty-four years old and I take my job as a police officer very seriously...which is why I find it to be astounding that those guys could do to me what they did. Where was the respect I ask you? As I said it was exactly two months ago today. I was on a foot patrol in the Red hook area of Brooklyn and I had an hour to go before I went off duty. It was four thirty in the afternoon on a warm spring day in the month of May. Dressed in my tight fitting navy blue button down police uniform shirt, my navy blue clip-on tie, tight fitting navy blue police issue uniform pants, and black patent leather lace-up (clonky) shoes I was walking down a pretty seedy street when I happened to notice a homeless man in an alley behind a very rundown apartment building. He was lying on the ground against a row of those extra big, extra strong, metal garbage pails. My first instinct was to just ignore him and continue on my foot patrol of the area, but then I thought that perhaps he could be dead or maybe if not dead he had been the victim of an attack of some sort. God knows crooks and muggers are always preying on the homeless...they make such easy victims after all. One would think that a mugger would not prey upon a homeless person, but more times than not homeless people are carrying around a stash of money in the amounts that anyone would find to be shocking. I turned and walked slowly into the alley, my hand on my baton. When I was standing directly over the homeless man the smell he gave off assaulted my nostrils.

"*Whew...*" I said disgustedly, waving my hand over my nose and rubbing the tip of my highly shined black patent leather shoe against his leg. "Hey Bub, you okay down there?"

When he didn't respond I nudged him again with my shoe and he stirred slightly, letting out a loud and offensive sounding snort as he came slowly awake.

"Wha-whass th' problem???" the homeless man gasped as he opened his very bloodshot eyes.

I squatted down beside him despite the awful odor coming from him. He was a white male, approximately forty to forty two years old; he had a long and filthy beard, and reeked horribly of liquor, body sweat, and urine. I saw the empty bottle of scotch lying beside him and nodded my head disapprovingly.

"Wh-whasamatter Officer?" the homeless man slurred and tried to sit up.

He was dressed in sneakers that were all torn up and looked to be two sizes too big for him, an old pair of jeans with holes all over them, and a long rancid looking trench coat. I quickly surmised that he had found his clothing in people's garbage or at a clothing drop-off for the poor.

"Nothing is really the matter Sir..." I said to him as politely as possible. "But you can't be sleeping back here against those garbage pails. This is a residence and..."

"I ain't disturbin' nobody..." he spat drunkenly, cutting off my words in mid sentence. "B'sides, all these damn apartments in this crappy buildin' are empty... Fuckall, I wanted to sleep inside but the empty buildin' is all locked up. Now why in hell would they lock up an empty goddamn buildin' huh Offissher?"

"Still in all Sir and be that as it may, you'll have to move on..." I said with a smile.

As I squatted there he slowly got himself to his feet. When he was standing he looked down at me as I smiled up at him, still trying not to gag on the odor emanating from him.

"Jes' doin' your job I suppose..." he said. "I'll find me some other damn spot for the night..."

"There's a shelter for the homeless a few blocks up..." I said and stood up, facing him. "Why don't you go there for the night?"

"Shelter Shmelter..." he said angrily and spit on the ground, just missing my shoes. "I'll take my chances on the streets if it's all the same with you Officer."

With that he slowly walked out of the alley. I watched him go, a slight smile still on my face and a feeling of sadness for him and others like him in my heart. I was about to walk out of the alley also, but just then, from behind, I was bashed over the back of my head with what felt like a metal pipe of some sort.

"GRRnnfff..." I gasped horribly and saw my police hat go flying off my head before I hit the ground and fell into unconsciousness.

While my attention had been focused on the homeless man I hadn't noticed the two big burly men who had been in the back of the alley of the apartment building...obviously looking for someone to mug...or a cop to do a real number on. I surmised that their first target had been the homeless guy. More than likely they had planned to harass him a bit, maybe find out if he was one of those homeless people who secretly carried around bags packed with money. But when they saw the blond police officer make the scene I guess they figured that he would make a more appetizing victim. When I came to the first time I found myself missing my pants. I was wearing just my white briefs, my knee length blue nylon ribbed dress socks, my black patent leather lace-up shoes, and my shirt, unbuttoned all the way and my tie missing also. My gun belt, minus my gun and baton was still around my waist and my hands were cuffed behind me...with my own damn handcuffs I might add. Just for the record here, there's nothing worse for a police officer than to be captured and locked in his own handcuffs. I was sitting on the ground against the garbage pails where the homeless man had been sleeping not more than fifteen minutes ago.

"Wha-what happened?" I whispered as I came to, look-ing down at myself and seeing that I was no longer wearing my pants. "Wha-what the fuck is going on???"

Slowly, I looked up and saw two men standing over me. They were both pretty big and burly looking, a fiendish look on each of their faces. They were both dressed in worn looking jeans, tee shirts, and scuffed up construction boots. I also saw that my gun was in the waistband of the bigger guys jeans.

"You do as you're told Cop and you may live to see tomor-row and the day after that..." the bigger of the two guys said to me, my nametag that had been clipped to my shirt now in his hand as he held it up between his fingers. "Nevaready huh? That's a fucked up name to be tagged with Cop. Officer Fucking Nevaready was definitely never ready for us! HA, HA!!!"

The two men laughed stupidly at the big lug's joke where my name was concerned. Nothing new there huh? The guy dropped my nametag on the ground and smashed it with one of his huge booted feet. The sound of the plastic cracking was heartbreaking to me somehow.

"H-hey, what the fuck? That's my nametag you blasted scum!" I ranted up at the guy.

"Yeah? Well, you're lucky that I didn't pin it to one of those sweet looking tits of yours Officer Never Ready, whoops, I'm sorry, Nevaready that is," the huge guy said and spit on me, his phlegm landing on the side of my uniform shirt.

"FUCKER!" I snarled.

The other guy had my goddamned badge...he had it pinned to his shirt, SHIT!!

"Wha-what do you mugs want?" I asked them, my head still stinging from the blow it had been dealt. "I'm a police officer!! This is a fucking outrage, stripping me of my pants and restraining me...shit!!"

They looked at each other, smiled wickedly, and unzipped their jeans. I watched in absolute fucking horror as they both pulled huge, hung, erect cocks out of the fly openings of their jeans.

"Ohhhhh shit..." I croaked and pressed my back against the garbage pails, cowering there in fear. "Ohhh fuck, oh shit, you bastards!! Not this!! OH FUCK, not this!"

"You can yell for help if you want to Cop, but I doubt anyone around this neighborhood is going to come to your assistance..." the bigger of the two guys said to me with a mocking grin on his face.

I quickly looked down at my radio.

"We turned it off Cop...for purposes of privacy..." the other guy said. "It's just you and us here..."

The smaller of the two guys stepped over me, his big hard cock dangling mere inches from my trembling lips.

"I'll go first Ronald..." he said. "Seeing as I was the one who saw him first and came up with the idea to turn him into a fucking cheap pussy whore. Come on you beautiful cop, suck my big hard cock..."

"Go for it Alex..." the bigger of the two of them said, sounding rather stupid.

God, the sight of him standing over me with that horse-sized cock of his in my face and my badge pinned to his shirt was unnerving. I tried to move my head away from his huge cock but when I did move my head it began spinning. I was still reeling from the horrible blow from earlier. I could feel the lump forming already and wondered if I had suffered a concussion. The next thing I knew the guys cock was in my mouth. He began pumping it in and out of my craw with brute force, made me deep throat it a few times, slapped me in the face with it, and forced me to lick it all over real slowly and gently with the tip of my quivering tongue. He even made me tongue bathe his big hairy, raunchy, and stinking balls for him. He held me tightly by my ears, squeezing the fuck out of them as he forced his huge cock into my mouth over and over again. The rancid stinking tastes of his ball sweat and cock juice slid down my throat, awful of awful man. I could actually feel his damned cock throbbing with a life of its own in my mouth. As the guy named Alex fucked my mouth like crazy the other guy, Ronald, stood there watching in awe, his cock getting harder and harder between his legs. It was hanging out of his jeans like a big throbbing python, thickly veined and twitching. I sputtered like crazy and saliva spewed out of the sides of my mouth along with Alex's pre cum as he thrust in and out of the hole in my face like crazy.

"Oh yeahhh fuckin' hot chops you got there Officer..." Alex crooned, still holding me by my ears. "Real hot fucking chops."

"RRRmmmffff!!!" I sputtered, looking up at him with my eyes filled with utter hatred.

Then, after a while more he shot his load, right into my mouth.

"RRRmmmffff!!!!" I sputtered again as his juices filled my maw. "GGRRRRFFFF!!!"

I had no choice but to swallow his damned cum. It tasted awful, all slimy, and sour. When he was done creaming in my mouth he held tightly to my ears, his softening dick still in my mouth.

"Ohhh man Ronald, this cops mouth is fucking great..." Alex crooned, still pumping his manhood in my cum soaked mouth. "Fuckin' best idea I've come up with in a long time..."

He held tighter to my ears, told me to suck his soft dick, told me to poke my tongue tip into his dick slit, and stood there sweating in ecstasy as I did as I was told. He raised himself to his tiptoes and pushed his soft dick far back in my mouth until his jeans were pressed against my face, making me chow down on him. Then, with his dick still in my mouth the bastard pissed, forcing me to swallow all of that as well.

"Grrrfffff!!!" I ranted as he let go of my ears and pissed and pissed into my mouth.

"Oh man Alex; I can't believe you're fuckin' pissin' in his mouth..." Ronald guffawed. "That's a really fucking rotten thing to do to such a handsome officer of the law, using him like he was your own personal urinal..."

"Yeah, but just look at him gulping down my piss..." Alex quipped and the two men laughed hysterically.

When Alex was done pissing he pulled his dick out of my mouth, stepped away from me, and Ronald took his place.

"You fuckin...rrrmmmmfff..." I gasped as Ronald pushed his big cock into my mouth next.

"Bight me and I'll make you sorry Cop..." Ronald said as he began thrusting his big fat cock in and out of my mouth.

He was rougher about it than Alex had been, slapping my face hard as I sucked him harder and harder. He pulled my hair, forced me to lean my head to the side as he guided my mouth over his sweaty and stinking balls, and then forced his cock down my throat a few times, forcing me to gasp for breath. I looked longingly at my gun, tucked in Ronald's jeans, totally out of my reach. I had mistakenly pulled my legs up so that my feet were flat on the ground. As Ronald forced me to suck his monster sized cock I had pulled my legs up because Alex was squatting beside me and having a grand ol' time stroking my big dick... which he had yanked out of the fly opening of my briefs and to his disbelief (and mine) found it to be hard as a fucking rock. Fear hard I would call it, my cock was fear hard. No fucking way I was turned on by what those two mugs were doing to me... no fucking way, no how!!

"Fuckin' hot cop is really enjoyin' all this shit Ronald..." Alex quipped as he stroked my meat faster and faster. "Lookit at how hard this cock of his is. I'm goin' to get this big fucker to shoot a load or two or three for us..."

"Ohhhh yeahhh, you do that Alex..." Ronald crooned breathlessly. "I'm fuckin' gettin' close to shootin' *my* load right now..."

And then, Ronald, like Alex, shot a big white creamy load of man juice into my mouth. I again had no choice but to swallow a big mouthful of awful tasting cum. As Ronald forced me to wolf down his load of slop I felt myself about to shoot my own as Alex stroked me harder and harder and faster and faster.

"RRRmmmffff..." I roared as Alex didn't handle my cock all that gently.

I shot my load on the ground between my legs, my cock throbbing in Alex's fist as he milked it like crazy. I looked up at Ronald with hatred in my eyes as he let his cock slip slowly out of my mouth.

"Lucky you are that I'm not goin' to make you drink my piss like Alex did you fucking hot cop!!" Ronald said gleefully and again spit on my shirt.

Alex let go of my dick and I was able to catch my breath.

"Y-you bastards..." I said, looking up at Ronald and quickly looking at Alex still squatting beside me. "You fucking perverts!!! You goddamned shit for brains mother fuckers! I'm going to see to it that you two go to jail for the rest of your worthless lives for this shit!!"

"You know Cop, in the position you're presently in I doubt very much you'll be doing anything but what we tell you to do..." Alex said and squeezed one of my nipples real hard; twisting it like it was a bottle cap.

"Yowwwwchhh..." I gasped. "Fucker..."

"Because if you don't do what we say I could easily see you winding up not breathing," Alex added.

I gulped hard, wondering if when this was all over they would kill me anyway...

"Come on Ronald; help me get this big cop on his feet..." Alex said sternly. "I want to work on him some more... Looks to me like you were never ready for us Officer Nevaready…"

Seconds later I was standing between my two captors with my cock still hanging embarrassingly out of my briefs. Alex and Ronald were each sucking one of my big, pointy, pink, meaty nipples, rubbing their hands over my big chest and flat stomach, and occasionally giving my semi hard manhood a good yank or painful squeeze.

"Ohhhh shit, I can't believe this shit is happenin' to me…" I muttered miserably as they feasted on my nipples like crazy. "Fucking perverts…degenerated thing to do to a cop!"

As I stood there helplessly in my uniform minus my pants and my gun belt hanging uselessly around my waist I looked around the alley. I saw my pants and tie on the ground by the wall of the apartment building. My hat was still where it had landed when I had been conked hard on the head. When it felt like they were about to suck my nipples right off my chest they stopped torturing them. They went on running their hands over me though, squeezing my muscular arms, slapping my flat stomach hard, and even giving my poor cock a good hard stinging rap every few seconds. That really got a good gasp out of me every time they did it. Then, Alex grabbed my cock again and began stroking it hard a second time.

"Ohhh shit, you fuckers…" I gasped and pulled myself to my tiptoes.

"Going to make him cum again eh Alex?" Ronald asked his friend.

"Yeah, I figure I'll make him feel good for now because he ain't going to like what we have in store for him next…" Alex quipped.

"Arrrrrrhhhh shit, let me go already you fuckers…" I moaned breathlessly and helplessly gyrated my body as Alex stroked me more and more. "Ohhhh man…"

"Let you go Cop?" Alex asked me as he stroked my aching cock. "Man, we're just gettin' started on you."

Ronald squeezed one of my nipples and then I shot my load…again, all over the ground.

"Arrrrhhh yeahhh yeahhhh you fucking bastards!!" I grunted as I stood there shaking and trembling in forced ecstasy. "Fuckin' makin' me shoot my damned load of cop spunk..."

When I was done Alex let go of my dick and I stood flat on my feet.

"Good goin' Cop..." Alex said and snapped the elastic waistband in my briefs against my skin.

He did it again two more times then looked thoughtfully at my BVDs.

"You know what Ronald; I'm going to take these briefs of his as a souvenir." Alex said, grabbing the sides of my briefs and pulling them down to my ankles.

"Oh shit, what next?" I muttered miserably. "Maybe you'll want my damned stinking socks too..."

I stepped out of my briefs and Alex stuffed them into his jeans pocket.

"Stealing a cops under shorts Alex?" Ronald asked his buddy. "Man, you can't get much lower or raunchier than that..."

Laughing, the two men began slapping my hairless bubble butt hard.

"Arrrghhhh!!" I roared angrily.

As they slapped my ass harder and harder it caused my dick and balls to flop around like crazy in front of myself. And unbelievably, my dick was getting hard again...

"Stop this shit already you fuckers!!" I yelled as they slapped my ass harder and harder.

"Your orders are our commands Officer." Alex said and squatted down to pick up the metal pipe.

"Oh no..." I muttered and Alex rapped me hard across the back of my head a second time with the metal cylinder. "GRRnnnffff!!!"

With a look of utter pain and agony on my face I hit the ground, unconscious again. When I came to the second time I found myself up on top of one of the big metal garbage pails with my legs stretched out wide and tied above myself by the ankles to the metal rung of the fire escape above us. My hands were still cuffed behind me and now I was gagged with my tie stuffed in my mouth, a length of rope tied over it, jamming it tightly in my mouth. My gun belt was no longer around my waist. They had taken it off me and thrown it with my discarded pants. My head was again spinning in what felt like a reverse orbit and I could feel the second lump forming there.

"RRRmmmffff!!!!" I sputtered angrily as my head cleared a bit and when I realized the horrible position I was in.

My asshole was wide open and a ready target for my two captors. With my head really spinning now I saw the two of them standing there flipping a coin with their cocks still sticking out of the fly openings in their jeans. Those cocks were long, hard, and throbbing, ready for some good ol' fucking...and I was the damned fuckee...all trussed up on that garbage pail like a stuck pig for their perverted pleasure. It amazed me how erect they were even after having shot their loads down my throat earlier. Alex put the coin in his pocket and I didn't need three guesses to know what was going to happen next.

"RRRmmmfff!!!" I gasped, silently begging them to release me.

"I won..." Alex said happily as he walked over to me. "I get to fuck the cop first."

I watched in agony as Alex grabbed his hard cock in his hand. Slowly, he guided his throbbing hard on toward my open and gaping hole.

"GGGrrrmmmfff..." I wailed miserably.

"Oh yeah Cop, get ready for this..." Alex said breathlessly and plunged his cock into my hole, without any type of lubricant whatsoever.

"RRRmmmfff!!!" I wailed in total pain as Alex began pumping his cock in and out of my hole like crazy. "MMMfff..."

"Good fucking thing you decided to gag him for this Alex..." Ronald said. "The way he would be screaming would definitely attract attention."

"Yeah, it sure would Ronald..." Alex grunted as he went on fucking me. "...Ohhh shit, this damn hole of his is so warm and tight Ronald...I could fuck this cop for hours..."

Alex grabbed my calves, ran his tongue over one of my socks, and fucked me harder and harder, thrusting deeper and deeper into my hole.

"Mmmfff..." I whimpered with my eyes squeezed tightly shut.

"Oh man, I'm gettin' close already Ronald..." Alex gasped and then spewed his juices into my hole. "Ohhh yeahhhh yeah-hhh!!!"

Alex rapped me hard across the ass cheeks as he came and came in my hole, drenching it with his cum.

"RRRmmmffff..." I gasped when I felt Alex's hot juices in my hole.

Alex pulled his spent dick out of my hole and Ronald quickly took position at my waiting most private crevice.

"RRRmmmffff!!!" I roared wildly and thrashed on the garbage can as Ronald grabbed his big hard dick and aimed it at my hole.

Ronald's dick was a lot bigger than Alex's and even though my hole was now lubricated with Alex's cum it still hurt like hell when Ronald rammed his dick into me.

"Ummmfff!!!" I groaned miserably and hung my spinning and aching head backward as Ronald began thrusting in and out of my poor hole.

"Ohhhh yeahhh Alex, you were so right, so fucking right..." Ronald quipped and grabbed my socked calves. "Fucking hot and tight hole he has..."

Ronald speared me like crazy with his big cock, making me sweat and sputter in agony. Saliva spewed out of the sides of my gagged mouth and ran down the sides of my face. All I kept thinking was, "Oh God, my hole, my poor hole, it hurts so bad what they're doin' to me..."

"RRRRR!!!!" I roared behind my gag.

"Oh man Alex, I'm goin' to fuckin' shoot my load already..." Ronald gasped, pumping my hole harder and harder. "Just can't fuckin' hold it back man!!!"

And then, I felt Ronald's hot juices flooding my hole as he came and came, panting like crazy, and squeezing my calves tighter and tighter.

"Ohhh yeahhh yeahhhh..." Ronald gasped breathlessly.

He pulled his dick out of my hole and the two men shook hands, congratulating each other on a great catch. My legs were aching miserably and numb at the same time as I laid there all stretched out and wide open on top of the garbage pail. A feeling of utter humiliation mixed with total rage enveloped me.

"Think you can go for another round of fucking this hot cop Ronald?" Alex asked his buddy, grabbing his cock in his hand at the same time. "He ain't goin' anywhere any time soon and he's all ours to do what we want with after all..."

"Sure can Alex." Ronald said happily and eagerly. "Man, by the time we're done with that hole of his he's goin' to have a sloppy cunt back there instead of an asshole..."

Alex laughed mockingly, stroked himself to a new hard on, and I rolled my eyes in disbelief and pain as he rammed his boner into my hole for a second round.

"RRRmmmfff..." I moaned weakly now.

"Oh man, I could probably fuck this damned cop over and over Ronald..." Alex said breathlessly as he pounded the shit out of my asshole. "What about you?"

"I'm ready when you're done Alex my man..." Ronald said, holding his giant cock in his hand.

I looked up at Alex with eyes filled with anger, hatred, and utter despair as he fucked me and fucked me and fucked me. Sweat dripped from my forehead and into my eyes, blurring my vision. A few minutes later Alex shot another load of hot cream into my hole. He pulled his cock out of my hole, stood there catching his breath, and then Ronald rammed his cock into my hole for a second round.

"Ohhhh yeahhh you fucking hot looking cop..." Ronald moaned wildly as he pumped my hole furiously. "Fucking beautiful like a goddamned blond woman would be...HAR, HAR for you Officer Never Ready!"

When Ronald came again into my hole he and Alex squatted down at my cum drenched maw and took turns licking it in and out like crazy, lapping up their cum that was in there.

"MMMMffff..." I sputtered with my head lolling back, the sensations of their tongues flicking around in my stretched hole driving me batty.

They even took turns sticking their fingers deep into my hole, seeing how many fingers they could get in there at one time. As the two men made sport of toying with my poor stretched asshole I closed my eyes again and my head spun.

"Fuckin' horrible thing to do to a cop..." I thought miserably and then felt Alex's dick ram my hole a third time.

I opened my eyes wide in disbelief and horror as the bastard fucked me a third time. DAMN, where did these guys get their energy??? It took a while longer for him to cum this time but when he did he again came in my hole, filling it with his juices.

"RRRRhhhhh yeahhh..." Alex screeched with his eyes tightly closed as he held onto my socked calves like his life depended upon it.

"GGGRRRmmmfff..." I wailed.

Ronald didn't go for a third round of fucking me at that moment but I knew they weren't done with me when I saw Ronald pick up my baton.

"Oh man Alex, I just came up with a real sick idea..." Ronald said my baton aimed at my gaping hole.

I shook my head no wildly from side to side as Ronald placed the tip of my baton against my cum soaked and wide-open hole. Slowly, he began pushing it in. When a good length of my baton was in my hole Ronald twirled it around in there, pumping it in and out of me.

"RRRmmmfff..." I whimpered horribly as Ronald fucked me with my baton.

Alex stood next to his buddy, watching in awe as he slid the baton deeper inside me. My head was spinning horribly now and I was feeling super lightheaded. Tears flooded my eyes and slid down the sides of my face. I was in total agony. Finally, Ronald yanked my baton out of my hole, dropped it on the ground, and he and Alex gave my ass cheeks a few good hard slaps with the backs of their hands. I squirmed on the garbage pail in pain as the slaps they were giving me got harder and harder with each blow. By the time they finally untied my legs and let me down off the garbage pail they had each fucked me one more time each. When it came to getting their cocks up their staying power amazed me. I knelt there in utter misery, my head spinning, sweating, crying, my legs numb, my hands still cuffed behind me, still gagged with my tie, and big droplets of cum dripping out of my asshole onto the ground. My hole felt all sopping wet and mushy. I knew it would be weeks before it felt even somewhat normal again.

"We goin' to let him go now?" Ronald asked Alex.

"Shit no Ronald my man..." Alex said in a breathless and fiendish sounding tone of voice. "I got a lot more ideas in store for this handsome piece of cop meat..."

I looked up at the two men through my tear-filled eyes and I thought I would pass out at that moment...

But before I had time to pass out Alex and Ronald hauled me to my feet by my upper arms... I wondered miserably what Alex had in mind for me next...

About fifteen minutes later I got my answer...I found myself hanging from the fire escape that was attached to the building we were in the back of...*and what a fucked up position I was hanging in*. Alex and Ronald had tied a good amount of rope around my upper arms and around my ankles, binding them tightly together. Then, they hoisted me up to the fire escape and hung me straight across the bottom of it by my tied upper arms and ankles. They added rope to my knees, around my calves, and around my chest to keep me secure on the fire escape. I hung there in agony like a piece of venison in a butcher's freezer.

"Man, is he a fucking sight or what?" Alex asked Ronald as they both looked up at me mockingly.

"Sure is." Ronald said, laughing. "That cop sure is in a shitload of trouble..."

"Come on; let's have some more fun with the handsome guy..." Alex said. "Fucking Officer Never Ready..."

They turned two of the big garbage cans over, stood up on top of them, and began lapping at my balls, applying horrible pressure to them.

"RRRmmmmmfffff..." I gasped as Alex and Ronald's tongues darted furiously over my poor gonads.

I balled my handcuffed hands into a big fist behind myself, sweated profusely, and hung my head down in total agony as the two men tortured my aching balls. I swore to myself that if it took me the rest of my life I would hunt these two down and kill them for what they had done to me. Then, they each sucked one of my by now swollen balls into their mouths and ran their tongues over them...harder than when they were just lapping at them.

"RRRmmmfff..." I sputtered and saliva spewed out of the sides of my mouth and landed on the ground.

I lifted my head and tried to look back at the two men as they sucked on my balls but my head was spinning again and I was forced to look straight ahead. When they started snapping their fingers against my wounded balls and slapping them I saw stars and practically did pass out at that point. Tears flowed uncontrollably from my eyes and I trembled like mad as they went on torturing me.

"Ummmmfff..." I whimpered as Alex ran a hand over my swollen and oversized balls.

"Okay Ronald, I think his balls have had enough." Alex said and gave my balls a final hard squeeze.

I yelped wildly, the two men laughed, and began untying the ropes holding me to the fire escape. When I was standing on the ground the two men stood at my sides squeezing my nipples, slapping my ass, and slapping my pecs hard.

"RRRmmmff..." I roared at them.

Alex took my tie out of my mouth and tossed it on the ground.

"F-fucking bastards...p-perverts you two are!!!" I yelled at them. "Fucked up thing to do to a cop... I will get you two for this, mark my words, BASTARDS!!!"

Alex picked up the metal pipe that he had rapped me with earlier and again hit me over the head...hard.

"GGGrrrnnnfff..." I gasped and hit the ground, unconscious.

When I came to a while later I found that I had been half tossed into a stinking garbage pail. My upper body was in the pail while my long muscular legs stuck out the side of it, dangling down.

"AAARRRHHH jeez, fucking bastards, goddamned rapists threw me in a garbage pail like I was so much refuse," I whimpered miserably.

The handcuffs were off my wrists and my gun was on top of my pants. Whimpering, crying, hacking from the stink in the garbage pail they'd left me in I wedged myself slowly upwards and out of the oversized receptacle. Balancing myself was difficult and I fell to the ground. With my head spinning and totally aching I crawled over to where my pants were. I thanked God and my lucky stars that they hadn't stolen my gun. Alex and Ronald's splooge was still dripping out of my asshole and my balls felt like they would never be the same again. When I got over to where my pants and gun were lying on the ground I sat up against the brick wall, wrapped my big arms around my legs, and cried tears of agony. I fucking howled in a guy's rage. After I got control of myself I managed to get my pants on over my shoes and socks, got myself slowly to my feet, and tucked my shirt into my pants. I put my gun belt around my waist and shoved my saliva soaked tie into my pants pocket. I found my badge on the ground next to my stomped on and crushed nametag. With my fingers trembling I clipped my badge back onto my uniform shirt. When I took a step to walk out of the alley my head spun wildly, my vision blurred, and I hit the pavement again...unconscious. When I woke up I saw the home-less man I had sent off earlier. He was standing over me, looking at me with a look of utter contempt.

"Pardon me Officer, but you can't be sleepin' here..." he

said to me. "This is a residence after all..."

I called in sick for the next three days after that. I went to a private doctor for an exam and never reported to my desk sergeant what had happened to me. The doctor found no concussion and said that other parts of me would eventually heal. There was no sign of any STDs (sexually transmitted diseases) and for that much I thanked God. I realize of course I should have reported it to my desk sergeant, seeing as Alex and Ronald could be out there preying on other unwitting cops, other Officer Never Ready's...but for the life of me I just *could not* report it. I simply told my sergeant that I had come down with a nasty virus and the doctor I had gone to gave me a voucher attesting to that. I never saw Alex or Ronald again...but I am still a New York City police officer...and damned proud of it...

The End

Officer Red P.

My name is Stan. I live in Brooklyn New York and work for the department of sanitation of New York City. I'm what most people would call a garbage man, great job title huh? Hey, fuck that, the pay is great but the hours leave a bit to be desired…that is up until recently when the hours became a blessing of sorts. Because I have to get up around four o'clock every morning for my start time on the job it makes sense that I walk the dog before heading off to work. Plus, I would not want my wife walking the dog at that godforsaken hour anyway. A quick walk for the dog in the nearby park, bring him home and then off to work for me in my dark green colored sanitation worker uniform, my garbage man uniform hardy har and har. I have to be at work at six AM to start my shift so getting up when I do insures that I'm on time everyday, but on the day that I want to tell you about herein I was a tad late getting to my job. So, I get up around four AM, do the three necessary S's, shit, shower and shave and then climb into my sanitation uniform of a clean white or black tee shirt, a lightweight green jacket, matching green work pants and clonky black lace-up shoe boots. My wife and I live a few blocks from a big park so that's where I take Simon to do his morning business. He piddles a bit along the way at stops along the sidewalk but it's in the bushes in the park that he really does his important productions hardy har and har. Once in the park I let Simon off his leash and let him scamper free to take care of himself. On the morning that I am telling you about here I saw a cop's car in the park. Obviously he had rolled in and down the ramp that was set up for such things. I wondered why the lone officer in the car would be patrolling the park at this time of the morning, night to some folks. There were never any occasions of drug dealing, killings or prostitution in the park, this was a pretty decent neighborhood after all. The cop was just sitting there, not really doing much of anything. I got Simon back on his leash and as I passed the cop car I saw that he had the inside light of his car on. He was a handsome dude, sitting there writing in his notebook. He glanced up at me through his open window and nodded. His deep blue eyes looked droopy. I guessed he had been on duty all night. His dark hair though was neatly combed. His police hat was on the passenger seat. I nodded a greeting at him, me looking half-asleep as well and he smiled politely at me. With Simon done with his business I went home to drop the dog off, kissed my sleeping wife goodbye, and left for work... This was the day that started it all...

During the next week the same thing happened again when I was walking Simon. I took the dog to the park and lo and behold there was the cop again. He was sitting there writing in his notebook and this time when I passed by his car I said "Good morning" to him. He said the same thing back, adding that it was cool to let the dog off the leash. I simply looked at him sitting there in his car, all decked out and handsome in his dark blue uniform complete with a tightly knotted tie. You don't find too many officers of the law who wear their tie with their uniform these days.

"Last time I saw you here you put the dog back on the leash as soon as you saw me," he said with a sly looking grin. "Its cool man, I won't ticket you for having the dog off the leash. Actually, there's no law that says you can't have the mutt off the leash."

I politely thanked him. He went back to his notebook under the inside light of his car and I let Simon off his leash...

It was another week or so later when I encountered the cop again. This time he was simply sitting in his patrol car with the inside light on, not writing in his notebook. As I passed his car and said "Good morning" to him he said, "So you work as a sanitation man huh?" I let Simon off his leash, he scampered off and I told the cop yes, I work as a sanitation worker. With a stupid looking grin on my face I asked him what gave me away. He said the uniform and the smudge of soot or whatever it was on the crotch of that day's uniform pants. I quickly looked down to where he was looking and noticed the smudge on my pants. The last time I had worn those particular pants some dirt from someone's garbage had spilled on me. I supposed that the wash hadn't gotten the smudge out and it was now permanently stained.

"Oh yeah, would you look at that?" I replied, running my hand over the smudge, noticing how the officer watched me do that. "I guess I'll have to change out of these uniform pants when I get home after walking the dog."

"Yeah, I suppose you'll have to," the cop said, tugged on his tie, and started his patrol car. "Have a good day Garbage man."

"You too Officer," I said and waved as he drove off, up the ramp and out of the park.

Jeez, as I walked Simon home that morning I realized I had a rage boner in my smudged uniform pants... He had called me "Garbage man" in a sort of condescending way. My cock boned up even harder...JEEZ...

The next week I saw the cop again. He was parked in the same place in the park. I realized that every week on certain days this was becoming pretty routine. As I walked past the patrol car I had Simon on the leash and I heard the cop say "Looks like the wash still didn't get that smudge out huh Garbage man?" I stopped for a moment, let Simon off his leash, and looked down at my uniform pants.

"Nah, looks like it didn't," I said, rubbed my hand over my crotch, gave it a quick squeeze as well, and walked off to supervise Simon.

As I walked home later on I thought how the cop seemed to be grinning when he mentioned the smudge on my pants that time. I wondered if he noted how I had not only run my hand over the smudge but also squeezed it as well. Before leaving for work

I used a damp paper towel to wipe off the smudge I had deliberately put on the crotch of my pants that morning. I thought how
he had to be looking real close to have noticed that smudge on
my pants, the only light being the light in his patrol car, the moon
above and a lamppost... And the second time he noticed it, it had
to have been through the rearview mirror as I approached his
patrol car with Simon on the leash.

That day while on the job making my rounds with my
buds in our stinky ass garbage truck I thought about the cop. For
whatever the fuck the reason I thought about him addressing me
as "Garbage man" and the next thought that filled my mind was
me on my knees and sucking his cock. Okay, I'm a married guy
but what the fuck? Some guys cheat on their wives with other
women, that's something I would never do. I myself have always
had a thing for guys in uniforms, something about the authority
that the uniform emanates. And if the guy wearing the uniform is
handsomer than fuck, well, that just moves me along even more
in the area of my crotch. And the cop was not bad looking at
all. With his short cut dark hair and blue eyes he looked kind of
muscular sitting in his patrol car. I guessed his age to be in the
mid thirties. But for me the biggest arouser was the policeman's
uniform. I supposed that that was where my fantasy of sucking
him off came from. He was a handsome fucking dude in a cop's
uniform and why the fuck not would I be wishing I could suck him
off? Anyway, everyday after that when I went out to walk Simon
I deliberately made a smudge on my "Garbage man" uniform
pants with some melted chocolate. The stuff was easy to wipe
off once I got home, but it sure would give my cop something to
comment on where my crotch was concerned. This time when
I saw him sitting in his patrol car we smiled at each other and
looking at my crotch he told me again how my uniform pants
were smudged, calling me "Garbage Man" yet again. I told him
that I knew and that for whatever the fuck the reason the smudge
just wouldn't come out. He grinned and nodded his head as I let
Simon off his leash to scamper in the park and do his business.
While Simon was frolicking around in the park I and the cop chat-

ted for a while. I had asked him why he was in the park every once in a while and he said it was the perfect place to catch up on his tedious paperwork. Glancing at my smudged crotch from his seated position he asked me why I was up so early. I explained how my "garbage man" shift started real early and the dog did need to be walked.

"Simon," I said, nodding toward the dog as he made his way in the bushes.

As we were talking I saw that the cop had moved one hand down and over his crotch and I swear it looked like he was playing with himself. Fuck that, it didn't look like he was playing with himself, *he was playing with himself.* I was standing right next to the window and with the inside light on in his car there was no hiding what he was doing at that moment. My breath caught in my throat. Then, he abruptly told me to have a good day and drove off...

While I was at work that day collecting garbage in the neighborhood where I was stationed all I could think about was my cop. It was funny how he coined me with the term "Garbage Man" and I had come to think of him as "My Cop." I decided that day that the next time I saw "my cop" I was going to make a move for him...

So, about a week later when I got to the park with Simon I saw the cop's patrol car parked in the usual spot. I hadn't seen him in a few days and was wondering if perhaps he had decided on another spot somewhere else to do his paperwork. This time I didn't have a smudge on my pants but the bone hard erection I was sporting in my "Garbage Man" uniform trousers was evident as all hell while we chit chatted, me and "My Cop." My erection was even more evident for the fact that I did not put on any under shorts that day, but it was to be "My Cop's" under shorts that turned out to be the fancy of the day let me tell you. As we chit chatted and as he stole glances at my plumped up crotch he grinned and said, "No smudge today "Garbage man." I smiled down at him, saw that the fly on his uniform pants was open and said, "No, uh, no smudge today Officer." As I looked down at his

unzipped uniform pants I could see that he was wearing some
sort of red underpants under his uniform pants. It was obvious
now that we were both checking out each other's crotches. As
for myself I was practically drooling at that point. Fuck, I had a
feeling what his red under shorts was and if I was right it made
my heart thunder in my chest. What was in those red undies was
pulsing like crazy. I could see it throbbing. After some more general conversation I took a deep breath, looked down at his open
fly and said, "Bet you can't wait to get home to the wife huh?"
He chuckled, tugged a bit at the pouch of his red under shorts
so that they were sort of sticking out of his fly now and said that
yeah, he would be heading on home but fuck of all fucks the wife
would be sound asleep. Glancing up at me he asked if my wife
was sound asleep as well when I returned from walking the dog. I
smiled from ear to ear, knowing all too well where all this wife talk
was going and said, "Yeah, she's sound asleep when I get back."
"My cop" tugged some more on what I saw was now some sort
of silky material that was sticking out of his uniform pants and
said that he would have to make do with his right hand when he
got home, said right hand tugging now at the tip of his pre cum
oozing cock in his red undies. I laughed softly and plunged on
in by asking him if he needed a hand. We looked at each other
in silence. Simon was sniffing around at my feet. Fucking dog
always had a thing for my clonky shoe boots. My wife thought
it was just so "fucking cute" whenever the dog would lick and
sniff my footwear. The cop whispered up at me, "I need more
than a hand "Garbage man," I need a goddamned mouth." As
he said it we were both glancing around the park, I supposed to
make sure that the coast was clear as would have been said in
old-time movies. There was nobody else in the park at that time
of morning but we needed to be sure right? As a cop and as a
sanitation worker we were both official city employees. What we
were about to embark on would not look good for either of us if
we were caught. We were still staring at each other and then he
made his way out of the car. He was very tall, at least six feet or
a bit more of musculature. He towered there in all his uniformed

glory, that patch of red sticking out of his fly. I could not believe that my fantasy was about to be realized. I was about to suck off a hunky muscle bound handsome cop. Simon licked "My Cop's" shiny lace-up shoes a few times and scampered off.

"Fucking dog, he loves licking shoes and boots," I said to "my cop."

"What about you "Garbage Man?" "My Cop" asked me. "Do you like licking things too?"

The cop reached into his car and turned off the inside light so that now only the moon and a lamppost lit our way. Standing there I placed a hand over the bulge in his red undies that was sticking provocatively out of his uniform pants. His cock was rock hard, really hot, and throbbing and so was "My Cop." He was REALLY fucking horny. His cock throbbed in my hand and more pre cum oozed against his silky feeling underwear. With a quizzical look etched on my face I trailed my fingers over his silky under shorts.

"They're my wife's used panties," he said as I ran my hand over the silky feeling garment he had on.

With my hand on his crotch we looked deep into each other's eyes. *His wife's panties? He was wearing his wife's goddamned panties?* I had heard of Wall Street suit guys going to work with their wife's panties under their thousand dollar designer uniforms, but a cop! Jeez, a cop who wore his wife's used panties... FUCKING HOT bud!

"They smell of her pussy "Garbage man", he said to me, reaching under my tee shirt, finding my pink fleshy nipples and giving them a squeeze and bottle cap twist each. "Makes me think of her having her scent all over my crotch. Now you're going to get to enjoy her scent too."

His look turned real intense as shockwaves of pleasure seared through me as he fondled and twisted the bejesus out of my goddamned man sized nipples.

"Oh fuck man, I just love a nice fat pair of titties "Garbage man," "my cop" huffed and squeezed my nipples harder, practically yanking me forward with them. "Bet your wife loves playing with these nubbies of yours huh?"

I let out a yelp of pleasure mixed with pain as he really gave my nipples the works with his big fingers... Then, he let go of my nips and stood practically at attention against the side of his patrol car.

"Pull my uniform pants down and suck my cop sized cock "Garbage man,"" he whispered breathlessly.

I didn't even look around for I knew he would keep an eye out. Jeez, not only was my fantasy of sucking a cop being made life but doing it in a public place made it all the more intense somehow. I slid to my knees in front of him and as I did so I unbuckled his belt. His gun hanging off to the side made my heart pound. Glancing up I saw that he was making sure I was not touching his gun or any other parts of his equipment. The only equipment I was to go for was what was packed in his wife's undies that he had on. When his pants and belt were down around his ankles I ran my hands up, slowly up and up his muscular legs, over his iron-like calves that were decked out in calf length blue cotton socks, his shapely thighs and then the prize I sought, his smooth tight ass in those frilly red undies. I squeezed his goddamned coconut shaped ass cheeks through the silk feeling underpants he had on and pressed my nose and mouth against the front of them. He moaned contentedly as I stuck out my tongue and ate his wife's pussy taste and his cock sweat off the undies.

"Oh yeah, you like that ass of mine huh "Garbage man?" he asked as I squeezed his ass some more, my hands filled with the silky feel of it. "Yeah, squeeze my ass and maybe if you get me off real nice I'll even let you eat it sometime."

I told him "Yes," that I loved his ass. Per his orders I told him how sweetly scented his wife's underpants were against his crotch. I licked the outline of his balls through the frilly panties. They looked to be a few sizes small on him but somehow that made it even more enticing. There was just something so sexy and vulnerable looking about this well muscled cop wearing a pair of his wife's underpants rather than a jockstrap or a pair of guy's under shorts. Then, the moment of truth arrived. I let go of his ass cheeks, lowered the red silk underpants in front, tucked them under his juicy smelly balls, and looked in awe at the meat stick that had been in there. His cock was truly cop sized, the way he had described it earlier. I glanced down at his baton on the ground as it stuck out of his belt and then at his cock.

"A regular nightstick I had in those frilly underwear's huh Garbage man?" he asked me as I leaned forward and devoured him into my mouth, my fingers trailing along his balls as I began the suck routine.

"My cop" groaned loudly as I took the red tomato head of his manhood deep into my craw. Damn I thought; I had a cop's cock in my mouth. This was riveting. I sucked it hard, suckling and drooling over his cock head. I poked my tongue into his wide sexy slit a few times and let me tell you that really got a few good grunts of pleasure out of him. I slobbered over his slippery shaft and again gobbled him into my mouth, ran my hands up and up his muscular legs again until they found his sexy ass cheeks. I pushed forward against his ass cheeks with my hands so that he was forced deeper into my throat. Fuck me I thought, I had "My Cop" moaning and groaning in his wife's panties. HAR!!!

I fondled his nuts some more, loving the feel of those kiwi sized knockers in my fingers almost as much as I loved his ass cheeks in hand. As he moaned and groaned things like "Oh fuck yeah, FUCKING A," he gyrated against his patrol car, force-feeding me his sausage now. With his cop-sized cock again in my mouth I sucked him back and forth like crazy. He made a mixture of whimpering sounds of joy mixed with the grunts of a soldierly sounding cop in the throes of wild abandon. With one hand I reached down to the ground and found his baton. He looked down at me in disbelief as I slid the baton upwards, toward his mouth.

"Kinky as me huh "Garbage man?" he asked as I slid the tip of his baton into his mouth. "OHHHHHH fruucckkk…"

As I sucked him I gently slid his baton in and out of his mouth. He drooled on it and without being told to he placed his hands behind his back…

"FRUUUCKKER…" he moaned as he ate the first few inches of his baton.

I knew he was getting close to shooting his load when the shaft of his cock in my mouth started pulsing like crazy. Fuck, I could actually feel the veins in his manhood plumping up as I sucked him. I tossed his baton aside and suddenly he was filling my mouth with his cop slop, splash after splash of his pearly juices filled my craw as he thrust in and out of my mouth, hitting his ass cheeks that I loved so much against his patrol car. He swore at me like a marine, demanding that I eat every drop of him. I swallowed and swallowed. Simon was standing nearby wagging his tail, seeming to be fascinated watching his master gulp down a cop's good stuff. While I was scoffing down his juices I wondered if what he said about a wife at home was really true. He had enough juice in him to fill me to the brim. This cop hadn't shot a load in some time that was evident. Maybe the frilly panties belonged to some slut he saw once in a while and who he hadn't seen in some time. When he was done and catching his breath I let his cock slip out of my mouth. I gave it a few kisses as it went soft and his balls as well as they hung real sexy over his wife's undies tucked under them. As I kissed his balls I ran my hands over the sides of his sexy lady under panties. He thanked me for the blowjob and watched wonderingly as I unlaced his shoes…

A short while later the cop was seated back in his patrol car but his wife's undies were now tucked in my "Garbage man" uniform pants pocket, a real kinky souvenir of the first time I sucked "My Cop" off. Ah yes, I still see "My Cop" on occasion and he still lets me suck him off. After that first time was done we both said how we had to get going, me to my "Garbage Man" job and he to go off duty. Fuck but that was a good way to start the day. While working that day I used the cop's wife's undies to wipe my brow whenever I started sweating…I sniffed them a few times and saw "My Cop's" handsome face in my mind as I did so…

The End

Tyrone
(A Cleeve and Otis Story)

Fuckers, *goddamned bastards!!!* They were at it again, pawing me, slurping on me, helping themselves to all the tender and exposed parts of my rock hard muscular body. This time there were five of them, count them, *five,* all white guys too, just like the last time. Two of them were standing at my sides, slurping wildly on my big fat nipples, sucking them ferociously, bighting them, licking them, and lapping at them like dogs in heat. I swear to God and all the angels in heaven those guys must have had bionic tongues. The way they were slathering their mouths on my oversized nips attested to that shit! Another two of them were kneeling in front of me, taking turns sucking my giant black cock, licking the veiny sides of it, pumping it alternately in and out of their greedy mouths. Fuck, these white guys knew how to get me just about to the fucking point of no return and then stop just in time, so I couldn't shoot my load, teasing the fuck out of me bud. Every time they poked their mangy tongues into my wide sexy piss slit they got a good loud moan followed by a grunt out of me. Fuck, they had already pumped two loads out of me and they were at the moment teasing and forcing me toward a third. It was a mesmerizing feeling let me tell you. I was all sensitive and sexy feeling from having just gotten off not all that long ago and now I couldn't decide if I wanted to cum again or just to have the white guys leave my damned meat stick alone. This was all too bizarre man. Fuckers loved watching me shoot my thick creamy loads for them. The second time I had cum they all took turns slapping my poor cock as I shot and shot my load. Fuck, every part of me was hyped up, sensitized, and alive, tingling like crazy. Fuck man, I was super sensitive to the touch after having shot two big loads. But these white boys wanted more, *and they were going to get it.* Oh fuck me hard and unbelievable they had paid for it after all. The fifth guy was kneeling behind me, licking and tonguing my big juicy plum-sized balls from behind me while he ran his hands over my tight round bubble butt, giving it a hard slap every once in a while. The sounds of slurping and eating emanated from the backs of my thighs as that fucker really chowed heartily on my big black family jewels. Every time he squeezed my sexy ass cheeks I felt completely humiliated. I was totally powerless to stop them from using me as a goddamned sex toy because I was shackled up good and tight in that weird wooden structure that Cleeve and Otis kept me in most of the time since they had captured me... (I'll tell you about that momentarily.) It was made out of four big pieces of heavy-duty lumber, all nailed together in the shape of a huge square. In each corner of the thing was a metal shackle, which could only be opened with a key. Cleeve and Otis were the only two who had keys for the damned things. Even the customers who paid to use me weren't allowed keys to release me. I supposed that Cleeve and Otis were afraid that some of the customers would take pity on the poor shackled muscle brute and set him free after using him. But Cleeve and Otis made sure that that would not happen, seeing as they needed me to bring in the bucks for them at the moment. I was standing in the square wooden structure in a stretched out spread eagle position shackled tightly at the wrists and ankles. And fuck me, but I was totally naked except for a pair of knee length (OTC to some feet fetishists out there) black nylon ribbed dress socks. Why I was wearing a damned pair of men's dress socks was still a mystery to me as the five white guys went on and on feasting feverishly on me. I grunted and groaned in a mixture of anger and ecstasy at the same time. All I knew was that Cleeve and Otis had each rolled one of the socks onto my feet before setting me up in the wooden structure for the white guys.

And then, fuck of all fucks, when the five guys arrived, Cleeve and Otis presented me to them as they ushered them into the room where I was kept. I watched as money was taken out of all of the guy's pockets and handed to Cleeve and Otis. And we're talking big bills here bud not just twenties and fifties mind you. My two captors counted the money and told the guys that they had just bought two hours with the black hunk. Black hunk is right. I'm black as the night, six feet tall, and then some, I have deep dark brown eyes, and short cropped hair. My body is super muscular and perfectly toned from all the grueling workouts I put myself through at the gym day after day. My hands are as big as hams, my arms are long and wiry and rock hard muscular, with biceps as big as bowling balls. My shoulders are as wide as a doorway. My stomach region has been described as a six-pack and trainers at the gym say that my legs are as strong as two tree trunks. I'm twenty-seven years old. My name is Tyrone Webber. The five white guys wasted no time stripping their clothes off and getting their hands on me. I swore at them, cursed like a sailor, a marine, and demanded to be released but they ignored me and went to work feasting on me. Cleeve and Otis always left the room while the customers were using me. Suddenly, one of the guys sucking my cock and the guy behind me working my balls decided to have a little nasty pulling party with my most private and most tender parts. They guy behind me started pulling my big balls back with his mouth, so far as to get them under my mangy ass crack while his nose was pressed up against my raunchy crack back there. As he suckled my balls in his mouth he breathed deeply in and out, sniffing heartily at my damned stink hole. The guy in front of me started pulling my cock forward with his mouth, sucking me hard and meanly at the same time.

"Ohhhhhh you fucking bastards!!!" I roared breathlessly. "Easy with my damned cock and balls!! Those aren't toys after all you mangy faggots!!"

The other guy who had been sucking my cock licked the side of it as his two buddies played tug-of-war with it. The other two guys went right the fuck on slurping heartily on my nipples, torturing them wildly.

"Fuckin' tit hungry perverts!!" I seethed. "Ahhhhhhhh shit, I-I'm goin' to cum again you bastards!!!"

And then, this time with no teasing, sure enough, I shot a third load...right into the guy's mouth who was sucking the fuck out of my cock. As I came the pain in my poor balls was immense...but the guy sucking them didn't stop for a second. "*AAArrrhhhh you fuckers...*" I moaned as I came and came the third time.

When I was done the guy who had been sucking my cock let it slip out of his mouth and the guy behind me stopped working the fuck out of my balls. The two tit suckers however, didn't stop for a microsecond. As I shot my load and even afterwards they went on and on slurping, sucking, and chewing and out rightly mauling my poor man tits.

"AYYYYRRRRR, my goddamned man tits always get real sensitive and sexy feeling after I've shot a load..." I seethed miserably as chills and thrills coursed through my being.

"Man, I'm horny as all hell," the guy who had swallowed my load said breathlessly.

I watched then as he crouched down and began slowly stroking his cock, aiming it directly at one of my socked feet. Now I knew why Cleeve and Otis had put the socks on me. These guys not only wanted to have some nasty fun with me; they were foot and sock fetishists as well. I had heard and read about guys like that, but could never understand the fascination they had for another dude's socked feet. Somehow I figured it was a world unto itself. And woe is me I had fallen into that world and being a victim of Cleeve and Otis I knew that I was about to get a first hand lesson in the fetish. The other guy who had been sucking my cock proceeded to do the same thing, aiming his hard cock while stroking it at my other foot.

"Arrrrhhhhhhhh...*perverts...*" I whispered angrily and looked down at the two men *still* slurping on my man tits. "Fuck you two, stop torturing my damned man tits already!!"

But then, the guy kneeling behind me pushed my ass

cheeks apart and plunged his tongue into my hole.

"Uhhhhhnnnnnn!!!!" I gasped breathlessly and my rock hard muscular body bucked forward. "Fuckin' eatin' my damned black raunchy hole..."

And that's just what he did, licking and kissing it like mad, poking his tongue far into it and flicking it around in there, his saliva dripping in it, filling it. My eyes crossed in my head as he greedily sucked his saliva back out of my mangy and sweaty hole. I grunted and groaned uncontrollably. The two men jacking off at my big feet were close to shooting their loads... I could tell by the expressions of ecstasy etched on their faces.

"Fuckers, your two cocks don't make up one of mine," I spat bitterly.

"Maybe not you hot sexy bastard, but you're the one chained up the way you are," one of the guys said and snapped the elastic in my left sock.

"And goin' no where either..." one of the guys who had been slurping one of my nipples said and gave my exposed nipple a good hard slap.

He quickly slurped my nipple back into his mouth. I watched the two guys at my feet shoot their loads all over the long black socks I was wearing.

"Ohhhhhhh yeahhhh, yeahhhh, fucking A!!!" they moaned in unison, spraying and shooting their loads all over my socks.

I have to admit that there was something very erotic and sexy about the way their white cum slid down the black nylon socks. I could even feel the heat of their juices as it splattered on my socks they were that thin. Somehow the idea of this so-called male foot and sock fetish was arousing me. The only thing was I didn't want to be in the position I was presently in to be learning about it. Then, the two guys went to work licking their cum off the socks, sucking my big toes every few seconds through the thin nylon material.

"Shit, among everything else you're damned foot freaks," I said, watching them lick and lick my socks.

As they sucked and lapped at my toes and while the

other two ate my man tits more and more chills coarsed through me...

When their two hours were up I felt totally exhausted. They had forced me to shoot another load and the two guys and the guy behind me all shot their loads on my socks also. I was a totally beat to shit guy and stinking of their saliva, cum and sweat as they got dressed. I stood there with my head hanging down, totally worn out also from having been stretched out and shackled for more than two whole hours. I was dripping sweat, grunting when Cleeve and Otis came in. They said that they hoped that the guys had all enjoyed themselves and told them that they could come back soon if they wanted to. I didn't say a word, only because I would have been ignored anyway if I did. The five guys thanked Cleeve and Otis over and over and then left. When they were gone Cleeve and Otis came over to me. I looked up at them as they slowly approached me.

Ohhhh no, not again you two," I pleaded breathlessly. "Come on, those guys really worked me hard..."

"So they did," Cleeve said and stepped behind me.

I heard his zipper pulled down and then he rammed his big tool in my hole.

"ARRRHHHHHH!!!!!" I cried out in anguish.

After Cleeve and Otis each took a turn fucking the tar out of me it was time to take me out of the wooden structure and put me to bed. They each released one of my hands and grabbed my arms tight before I could do anything.

"Uuuuurghghhhhh!!!" I seethed through clenched teeth as they yanked my muscular arms painfully behind me.

I choked back tears of anger and total frustration as I felt the ropes being wound around and around my brawny wrists. When my hands were securely bound behind me Otis held me balanced by my upper arms as Cleeve unshackled my feet. He left the cum smeared socks on me as he pushed my very smelly feet together and proceeded to rope them tightly together also. When my feet were tied Cleeve grabbed my ankles, told Otis he was ready and Otis held my upper arms tight. Together they carried me over their heads out of the room and to the room where I slept...*gawd,* strapped down to a long wooden table...

Now I'm sure you find all this very erotic and kinky but I assure you that it was beyond terrifying for an average guy like me. Granted what I just described to you is the stuff that a lot of erotic fantasies are made of. But this was no fantasy man this was real fucking life. It was the worst few days of my life. I felt like my ancestors must have felt, like a slave and totally violated. It had started out like any other Saturday night. I had a date with a girl who I had met a few weeks ago at a single's bar where I had been hanging out with a few of my buddies. Her name was Linda. She was beautiful. I had finally gotten up the courage to buy her a drink and after that it was magic, total magic. On the Saturday night we went out I took her to a fancy restaurant in the neighborhood she lived in. I had dressed to kill in a black double-breasted suit black spit shined alligator lace-up shoes, a white shirt, black and white silk tie, the works man. Linda wore a red clinging dress that accented her beautiful figure perfectly. After dinner we decided to take a quiet stroll through her neighborhood. I was sort of hoping to wind up back at her place. As we were walking past a park holding hands she stopped and looked at the park.

"I love this park Tyrone," she said to me softly. "You want to know why?"

"Sure," I replied, holding her hand tight.

"See that park house all the way on the other side of the park?" she asked me.

"Yeah, isn't that where the public bathrooms are?" I asked her.

"Yes it is," she said, sounding sexy and put her arms around my big neck. "It's also where I want you to make love to me."

She pressed herself against me, causing my cock to grow hard in my suit pants. I couldn't believe what she had just asked me to do.

"I think you had too much wine with dinner," I said to her with a smile.

"I'm very serious Tyrone," she said. "It's been one of my fantasies since I can remember."

"*One of your fantasies?*" I asked her. "Baby, I can't wait to find out what the other ones are."

"You mean you'll do it?" she asked me hopefully.

"Sure will Baby," I said and we walked hand in hand into the park.

I wondered how lucky a guy could get. Not only had I met a beautiful woman, but she was a freak as well. In the big deserted park house we made love on the floor in the space between the men's and ladies room. My pants and underpants were down around my ankles and Linda's dress was pushed up above her crotch area. She rode my monster-sized cock like crazy, moaning and groaning in a passion I never saw in any other woman in my life. I was sweating like crazy laying there on the concrete floor as the girl made me shoot my load repeatedly into her hole, squeezing my cock with her pussy lips real tight. By the time we were done I was exhausted but Linda was only just getting started. She pulled herself off me and stood up, straightening her dress. Fuck, there really was something erotic about doing it in a public place. Besides beautiful and sexy the girl was more than erotically creative, totally fucking freaky.

"Come on, lets go to my apartment and I'll tell you more of my erotic and sexy fantasies you handsome devil," she purred.

I smiled up at her.

"I have to pull my pants up first you crazy girl," I said softly.

Linda giggled, told me to meet her in front of the park, and dashed out of the park house.

"Hey get back here!!" I yelled to her, a big shit-eating grin on my face.

I lay there laughing; my pants and briefs still down around my ankles. As I was about to get up two big white guys came into the park house and loomed menacingly over me.

"Told you there was a black hunk in here Cleeve," one of the guys said.

"Right as always Otis my man," the one named Cleeve said with satisfaction.

"H-hey, who are you two?" I asked them, propping myself up on my elbows.

At first I thought that they were plain-clothes policemen but something told me that they definitely *were not*. Then I thought that they could have been rapists who were after my girl. But even that for some reason didn't seem plausible here. I hadn't registered yet on a conscious level how they were looking at *me, really drinking in the sight of me* and with all my good stuff hanging out at that, jeez. They were both dressed in worn looking blue jeans, flannel shirts, and big clonky mustard colored construction boots. They looked like over-sized construction workers actually. Suddenly, lying there with my most privates of parts totally on display didn't seem all that kosher...

"Look guys, I can explain all of this..." I began to say with half a grin on my face, reaching for my pants and briefs at the same time. "You see, that girl out there is my date and she had-er-has, this erotic fantasy thing and... RRRMMMMFFFFFF..."

My words were suddenly cut off as the bigger of the two guys (the one named Cleeve) reached down and with lightning speed crammed a wadded up and smelly white rag into my mouth. Startled, I went to reach for the rag, intent on getting the foul thing out of my craw, but it was then that the two men each grabbed one of my arms and hoisted me roughly to my feet. My pants and briefs were still down around my ankles, the tops of my sheer black calf length socks showing. My flaccid cock swung back and forth over my dangling balls.

"RRRmmmfffff!!!" I sputtered into the gag, looking wildly back and forth at the two men in total confusion as they held me in a tight grip. "mmmmfffff..."

"Come on Otis, let's take this handsome black Romeo here to the van and get the fuck home," the one named Cleeve said in a fiendish tone of voice. "I can't wait to get a taste of his black meat..."

Jeez, what I thought was first a mugging and then a rape

attempt on my girl was definitely not the case here. These two white dudes were out to kidnap a black dude, and they had found their mark...*me!* They lifted me off the ground by my upper arms, swung my legs forward, and then back, then forward, and then back again until they got a good rhythm going.

"Hrrrmmmffffff!!!!" I gasped as they swung me back and forth, causing my long legs to fly outward and backward each time they propelled me back and forth over and over.

Then, at one point when my legs were stretched out in front of me they each caught one of them in their other hand while they held me aloft with one hand each.

"Mmmmfffff!!!" I squealed as they held me aloft now between themselves, seemingly effortlessly at that. "RRRMMMFFFF!!!"

They carried me by my arms and legs out of the park house. My struggling was in vain man, seeing as these two dudes were stronger than strong. When we were outside they quickly carried me out the back way of the park, unseen by any-one, even unseen by Linda. Looking helplessly to the side and in the fading distance I saw Linda waiting for me at the other side of the park. She was standing there with her arms folded, probably thinking that I was on my way over to her. Instead two maniacs were kidnapping me and I still didn't have any idea of why. I mean, they hadn't tried to take my wallet so I wasn't being mugged. FUCK, the only thing being stolen was *me...*

Moments later Cleeve and Otis had me in the back of a big van, which had been parked near the deserted park. Neither Linda nor I had noticed it earlier; we were that hot and that intent on our sexual goal. The two men had chained my hands above me to the ceiling of the van and also tied a good length of rope over the smelly rag in my mouth, securing it firmly in place. I watched helplessly as they untied my shoes, pulled them off my size eleven and a half feet, and then yanked my pulled down pants and briefs off me, their mouths dangerously close to my semi hard cock. They carelessly tossed my clothes aside and ran their big mangy hands over my long muscular tree-trunk like legs, snapping the elastic in my black sheer socks a few times.

"Good catch Otis, as always," Cleeve said mockingly, gripping the topmost part of my sock, caressing my calf. "And look at the size of his goddamned feet. Those guys we talked to who have that foot fetish for black guys are going to love this dude we nailed for them."

As always? What the fuck did that mean? Did these two guys do this sort of thing as a hobby or something? And what was that shit about the guys they had talked to who had a foot fetish for black guys? Where did my goddamned feet come into play where this was concerned? Then, without another word Cleeve did what I knew he was about to do...he slurped my cock into his mouth and began sucking it...*hard*.

"mmmmfffff..." I gasped and bucked forward.

As Cleeve sucked the fuck out of my cock the guy named Otis lapped at my balls, applying pressure to them with his big tongue. I fleetingly wondered if Cleeve could taste Linda's pussy juice on my cock. I mean, it hadn't been all that long ago that I had been inside her sugar walls. As I thought about Cleeve eating Linda's stuff off my cock some part of me churned with jealousy. The two men ran their hands up and down and up and down my legs as they feasted on my cock and balls. I was appalled to say the least. Never before, not ever in my life had I had sex with any man...but in the next few days I would have sex with many men... Even though I had already shot a load or two (with Linda) Cleeve and Otis managed to get me to shoot another two. I couldn't believe it to tell the truth. When they were done sucking me and working my balls they stood up at my sides.

"We'd better get rolling," Cleeve said to Otis. "We have a long drive ahead of us."

"RRRMMMMFFFF!!!" I roared loudly in a panic.

It had just been confirmed for me. *They were going to kidnap me...* Goddamn it but what was this all about???

"Yeah, that's right Dude, you're comin' with us," Cleeve said and tugged on my necktie. "But don't worry, you'll be well taken care of..."

Laughing, they both gave me a hard resounding slap on

the ass. I watched helplessly as they then stepped out of the van, closed the back doors, and locked them. The sounds of those doors being locked set my heart thundering still more in total fear. I stood there in utter darkness as the van started moving a few seconds later.

"Mmmmffff..." I sputtered madly as the vehicle picked up speed.

We drove for what felt like an hour or so and then the van stopped. When the back doors were unlocked and pulled open I saw that we were on a deserted road somewhere, the only lights coming from a lone lamppost on the road.

"Fuck man, I need another good taste of that dark meat before we get home Otis," Cleeve said as he climbed into the van.

"Me too Cleeve, fuck, me too," Otis said merrily, climbing in behind Cleeve.

Together they squatted at my sides and this time Otis sucked my cock as Cleeve tongued my balls.

"Mmmmffff..." I gasped wildly.

Again they ran their big mangy hands up and down my legs as they feasted heartily and with total gusto on my cock and balls.

"GGGRRRmmmmffff!!!!" I roared angrily at the total indignity of all this.

I had shot more loads than ever before in one night at that point and now these two were forcing me helplessly toward another... man was I aching. When I came Otis greedily gulped down my juices.

"MMMffffffff!!!!" I gasped loudly and arched my back as I shot my spurts in Otis' mouth.

Cleeve lapped at my balls, which were aching and swollen at this point. I wondered if Linda had gone looking for me. Probably she thought I had chickened out on our date and stood her up. Or maybe she thought I had been abducted and called the police. Right, fat chance of that. When I was done shooting my load Cleeve and Otis stood up again at my sides.

"I think we can take this gag out of his mouth at this point," Cleeve said and undid the ropes around the smelly rag in my mouth. "There's no one around here to hear him if he yells for help..."

Cleeve pulled the rag out of my mouth and I quickly licked my dried lips...

"Y-you bastards!!" I seethed, my chained hands balled into fists. "What's the point of all this??? You fuckers have kidnapped me!!! This shit is against the law!!! And what you've done to me, shiiiiit, that's out right rape!! By the time I get done with you two there won't be enough left to fill an empty coffee can!! I work as an assistant to a very prominent and very powerful lawyer!!! After you're arrested and in court he will make short work of you two! See if I'm kidding! You two won't have a snowball's chance in Hell!!! And furthermore...mmmmmmmffffff!!!!!"

Cleeve crammed the rag back into my mouth and retied the ropes over it again.

"Looks like we'll have to keep him gagged a while more," Cleeve said, looking at Otis in disbelief. "Fuck, of all things, he has to be a lawyer's assistant. No doubt our stud here is practicing to be a mouthpiece himself."

They then undid my necktie, slipped it off me, unbuttoned my shirt, and looked over my muscular chest, inspecting it, really taking in the sight and magnificence of it, practically drooling over the sight of it.

"Oh man, let's get this slab of beef home Cleeve," Otis said and squeezed one of my nipples hard.

"RRRRMMMFFFFF!!!" I gasped at his touch.

The two men again exited the back of the van, leaving me alone in the dark. The van started moving and we were again on our way...

Another hour or so passed and then the large vehicle slowed down, made a sharp turn, and slowly moved into a parked position. I had the feeling we had entered a garage. When I heard the two men vacate the front of the van and begin approaching the back my heart pounded in total fear. We had obviously arrived at wherever the hell they had intended to bring me. The back doors of the van opened and the two men stood there leering at me. I saw that we were in a very well lit garage.

"Well Stud, we're home," Cleeve said mockingly. "And for the time being so are you…"

"RRRMMMFFFF!!!!" I sputtered and reeled.

The two men climbed into the van undid the shackles around my wrists, and they each grabbed one of my arms in a tight grip. I couldn't struggle much because my arms were all numb from being stretched above me for so long during the ride…and Cleeve and Otis were two of the strongest fuckers I had ever met. They managed to get the top portion of my suit off me and then, holding me by my arms they brought me through the garage and directly into the house. I was wearing just my calf length black sheer socks and the gag that was still tied into my mouth.

"RRRMMMMFFF!!!!" I gasped and grunted loudly.

As we made our way through the house my cock hung long and semi hard between my legs. Cleeve and Otis enjoyed watching it swing from side to side as they moved me along.

"Damn, hottest fucking cock I've seen in a long time Otis," Cleeve said. "We are going to make a bundle with this fucking guy."

Make a bundle with me? Just like the questions I had about the guys they mentioned with the foot fetish for black guys I had to wonder what they meant by that. How in hell were they going to make a bundle with me? Or more to the point, did I really want to know? The house seemed to be the size of a mansion. I took in the sights of long hallways with lots of closed doors, lots of over-sized expensively decorated rooms and stairwells that led up and down to more rooms not within my view. Who the fuck were these two guys??? They brought me to a room in which the only piece of furniture was a long wooden table. It looked like it was made of solid oak. On the sides of it I saw that it had heavy-duty leather straps attached to it. I didn't need three guesses to know what Cleeve and Otis planned to do with me at that moment. They hoisted me up onto the long table, stretched me out on my back, and quickly strapped me down good and fucking tight. Cleeve took the gag out of my mouth again.

"Damn it you two!!" I yelled. "Why the hell have you done this to me???"

"What's your name Stud?" Cleeve asked me, looming menacingly over me, hard lust showing in his steely eyes.

"T-Tyrone Webber," I said sheepishly. "My name is Tyrone Webber. Now look, I'm not rich or nothin', I'm nobody famous or overly prominent, I'm just an average working dude, so if you're thinking about getting a ransom for me..." Cleeve smiled maniacally and squeezed one of my nipples, *hard.*

"Owwwwww!!!!" I yelped. "Easy with the man tits guy, they're two of my most sensitive parts..."

"That's good to know Tyrone," Cleeve said and squeezed my other nipple just as hard, getting another good yelp of pain out of me. "The boys will be glad to know that too."

"What boys??? Now listen, I'm not gay or nothin' so you really grabbed the wrong guy," I said, trying desperately to reason with them. "And what was that crap about my damned feet and a fetish and..."

"On the contrary Tyrone, we grabbed the right fucking guy," Otis said, giving my big cock a few strokes. "As Cleeve said you're going to make us a bundle...and may I say I like this bundle you got between your legs here..."

Cleeve took an unmarked spray can out of his jeans pocket, pointed it at my nose and mouth, and sprayed a goodly amount of its contents at me.

"Ohhhhhhhhhhh..." I grumbled at the awful scent and then I was in a sleepy stupor.

The next morning I awoke to the sound of the door to the room I was in opening. I didn't even have time to lay there awake and try to make some sense out of all this. But then, what sense would I have expected to make of this? I had been kidnapped and that made no sense to me whatsoever. My body ached from having been restricted by the heavy-duty straps for the entire night. Cleeve and Otis walked in together. They were both wearing black leather shorts and black engineer boots. Their bodies, *my God*, their bodies were works of art man, muscular, toned, and lean. It looked like they spent every free moment they had in the gym lifting weights. They both would have done any artist, photographer, or painter proud as models for their art. Cleeve was carrying a plate of food along with a fork. Otis stepped up to the table I was strapped to, leaned over my hard, throbbing, piss filled cock, and gobbled it greedily into his mouth.

"Ohhhhh shhhhiiiiitttt, g-good morning to you guys too…" I gasped, writhing in a mixture of morning ecstasy and humiliation under the binding straps.

"Breakfast time Stud," Cleeve said, setting the plate of food down next to my head.

Cleeve held my head up off the table by the back of my big sexy neck and fed me scrambled eggs, whole-wheat toast, and thin strips of bacon. Now let me tell you here, just for the record, I was never fed by a man before. Fuck, I was never fed by anyone before, especially while having my cock sucked at the same time. I found it difficult trying not to choke as the food slid down my throat.

"Ohhhhhhhh shittttt, fucking guy can't get enough of my big black cock," I grunted breathlessly in between being fed.

When I was done eating Cleeve set the plate aside, let go of my head, and anxiously slurped one of my nipples into his mouth.

"Uhhhhnnnnn…f-fucker!!" I gasped loudly. "Ea-easy with the damned man tits…told you they're two of my most sensitive parts…"

I belched loudly…

The two men ran their hands all over me as they feasted on me like crazy… I was breathless…

"Ohhhhh shiiittttt you guys, g-getting close now you fuckers…" I grunted through clenched teeth.

Then, when I couldn't hold it back any longer I shot my

load. Otis pulled my cock out of his mouth, held it tightly in his hand, and made me shoot my sexy load all over my stomach, my chest, and my nipples, which Cleeve had vacated just in time.

"AAAARRRRhhhh yeahhhhh, ohhhhhh fuck yeahhhhh!!!!" I roared loudly and bucked madly under the straps as I shot gobs upon gobs of white milky sperm all over my well-muscled body. "F-fuckers!!! Makin' me cum like crazy!!!"

The two men watched in awe, as it seemed to go on and on, my cock erupting like a damned volcano.

"Goddamn," Cleeve whispered. "Fuckin' guy is a gusher and then some..."

When I was done Otis let go of my cock and it flopped semi hard and beefy against my thick bush of black curly pubic hair, landing just under my belly button. The two men leaned over me, stuck out their tongues, and greedily sucked and slurped my man juices into the mouths, feasting on me all over again at the same time.

"OHHHH Damn..." I gasped as a tingling sensation coarsed through my muscular body. "Eating *your* breakfast now huh guys?"

My muscular rock hard body under the straps was glistening with my cum and sweat, jeez, what a sight I was...

When they slurped my cum off my nipples they again sucked and suckled them like crazy, bit on them, chewed them, and licked the very fuck out of them.

"Fuckers, easy with the man tits, they're two of my most sensitive parts," I whispered, repeating myself pleadingly.

When they were done they looked at each other across the table I was on.

"Man oh fucking man, we can't let this one go all that soon Otis," Cleeve said with determination in his voice. "God knows how much money we can make with him..."

"Not let me go all that soon???" I echoed Cleeve. *"What the fuck does that mean man??? My God, how many other men have you pulled this shit on anyway???"*

"You know Tyrone, you have a big fucking mouth," Cleeve

said, leering down at me. "So if you don't want to be gagged again I would shut that trap if I were you..."

He looked at Otis again.

"I agree with you man," Otis said to Cleeve. "I'll make some phone calls right away. I remember a few of the guys saying that they would just love to sample a hunky black guy some time soon..."

"Fuckers," I whispered in anguish.

A little bit later Cleeve and Otis brought me to the bathroom, leaving me alone in there. When they had undone the straps holding me to the table and hefted me off it by my upper arms I didn't have the power to struggle all that much. Being strapped down to a table overnight can really sap a guy's strength let me tell you. In the bathroom I pulled my black sheer socks off my feet and found all the necessary toiletries that I would need for a hot shower. As I stepped into the hot spray of water I glanced down at my socks on the floor and a feeling of utter anguish coursed through me, of all things, my socks, the only clothing they'd left me with... I thought again about what they had said about men and men's feet fetish. While I showered I also noted that the bathroom didn't have a window. I guessed that this was the bathroom that Cleeve and Otis had their victims use. No window, no means of escape, no way of summoning help... As I soaped up my muscular frame I thought about the fact that I had been fed a hearty breakfast and that I was being made to shower in a luxury like bathroom with all the necessities for being clean. I gathered quickly that I was not to be starved throughout this ordeal, nor made to smell like a homeless person...

When I was done in the bathroom Cleeve and Otis shackled me up in the wooden structure for the first time. I seethed angrily, now struggling like crazy in their grasps as they brought me to the room where the wooden structure was. I wasn't all numb any longer from having been strapped down all night. Now I was refreshed and agile, but still no match for my two captors as they half dragged half lugged me to the room where the wooden structure was. When I saw the thing and how it was designed I didn't need three guesses to know how I would be situated in it.

"Ohhhhhhh fuck, no, *no,* you guys," I blurted helplessly as they dragged me struggling over to the wooden structure. "Ohhhh shit, lookit that damned thing!!"

Once I was shackled up and helpless the two men again ran their hands over my chest, squeezed my nipples, smacked my six-pack stomach region hard, and tugged meanly on my cock and balls.

"Man, you are one hot lookin' dude Tyrone," Cleeve said breathlessly and gave my butt cheeks a good hard squeeze. "I almost wish we didn't have to share you with anybody, but we do need the money after all."

Otis gave my six-pack stomach another good hard resounding slap, getting a loud squeal out of me...

Laughing, the two men left the room, closing the door behind them. I stood there in total despair, thinking about my awful situation. I had no idea where Cleeve and Otis had taken me, except that it was far away from where they had grabbed me. I was totally powerless against them, and had no fucking idea if they would release me at all...if ever. I only knew that I was there to serve their perverted desires, and the perverted desires of the guys that would come and pay them to let them use me. At that last thought I struggled wildly but hopelessly against the shackles around my wrists and ankles. I wondered if Linda would have called the police by now...

The first group of guys showed up on Sunday, late in the morning. Cleeve and Otis ushered them into the room where I was. There were three of them, all white guys. They looked at me in awe before handing Cleeve and Otis stacks of fifty and hundred dollar bills. Watching them look me over in all my muscular nakedness I couldn't help a feeling of being on total display coupled with a feeling of total humiliation...

"Fucking hot lookin' black dude you got for us you guys," the first guy said eagerly to Cleeve and Otis.

"Yeah, he's hot all right," Cleeve said, glancing over at me. "He especially loves to have his big titties tortured."

I shot Cleeve an evil look and he winked mockingly at me.

Moments later Cleeve and Otis left the room and the three white guys gathered around me.

"Now look guys, this really isn't my scene," I began, my lips trembling. "If, if you know what I mean..."

Ignoring me they brazenly ran their hands over my big chest, squeezed my nipples a few times each, and stepping behind me, caressed the back of my big neck. They murmured things to each other like "Iron man, Iron chest, Nips hard like bullets, a neck like a bull," and so on and so on...

"Ohhhh fuck, FUCK, you guys," I moaned and groaned. "C'mon, give a guy a break here. For your sleazy information those two guys kidnapped my ass last night, right while I was out on a date with one of the most beautiful women in the world no less, no kidding!"

Then, two of them went to work on my nipples, slurping them into their eager mouths while the third guy turned my face toward him and forced me to pucker my thick sexy lips.

"H-hey...wh-what the fuck're you doin' man???" I gasped in a high-pitched tone of voice as he squeezed my lips into a puckered position.

When my saliva began dripping through my forcefully puckered lips the guy wrapped his own lips around mine and began sucking on them, gulping down my saliva. He held me tight by the face as he sucked and sucked my lips, forcing my saliva from my mouth and into his.

"UUUHHHRRRRRRR!!!!" I grunted as they worked me over like I was a piece of meat.

As they sucked my big nipples and sucked my lips my cock grew hard and long between my legs, pointing straight up at the ceiling. What was up with that anyway? I was no damned faggot after all.

"F-fruckers..." I seethed through my puckered lips.

144

The guy feasting on my now saliva drenched lips stuck his tongue into my mouth, held me tightly by the back of what he had termed my big bull neck, and kissed me and kissed me and fucking kissed me. Fuck it all, I thought miserably, "I'm bein' given the kiss of death by a faggot…"

"Mmmmm…fuckin' guy's mouth tastes real great," he mused and resumed sucking my still puckered up lips.

The two guys sucking my nipples were taking turns reaching down and stroking my hard cock. Each time they would get me almost to the point of shooting my load they would stop, driving me crazy with frustration.

"UHHHRRRRRR fruckers," I gasped again through my puckered lips.

"Fucking guy wants to cum like the dickens," one of the guys sucking my nipples said mockingly. "Ha, we're driving him batty."

He stroked my throbbing cock three times and then let go of it. Sweat poured off me everywhere. I was now more than aching to shoot my damned load. The guys went on and on slurping my nipples like crazy and sucking at my puckered lips. Then, when one of the guys sucking my nipples gave my hard cock a few strokes I concentrated with all I had and finally shot my load.

"Uhhhhhrrrrrrr!!!" I roared as my cock flopped around with a life all its own, spraying and spurting my juices all over the floor.

"Fuck, what a monster-sized load this guy just shot," the guy who had been sucking my puckered lips said in astonishment as he still held tightly to my lips, keeping them puckered, my eyes rolling in my head. "You know guys, I just came up with a great fucking idea…"

He let go of my lips and squatted down in front of my semi hard cock.

"Come on you two, leave his tits alone for a while," the guy said, looking hungrily at my cock, at the way the veins in it were at the moment extremely pronounced. "Let's chow down on this

145

meat stick of his..."

"Ohhhhhhh no, no man, please, not right after I just shot my damned load you fuckers!!!" I ranted madly as the guy who had been sucking my lips now slurped my semi hardness into his mouth. "ARRRRHHHH GA-GAWD..."

I bucked my body forward as he sucked my sensitive feeling cock like crazy. The other two guys squatted down at his sides, awaiting their turns. "Let's see how many times we can milk this black dude, see how many times we can make him shoot his creamy load," one of the other two guys said before taking my now hard cock into his mouth next.

As they took turns sucking my big black cock they murmured things like, "big black meat stick, nice plump balls, balls as big as two ripe plums." The three of them sucked me and sucked me till I shot my load again, grunting and groaning and swearing at them like a captured marine, or more precisely a captured lawyer's assistant. One of the three white guys held my cock tightly in his hand as I shot yet another hefty load all over the floor.

"ARRRRRRRRR shhhiiiitttt," I seethed. "Fucking perverts!!! Ohhhhh MAN!!"

"Yeah, that's it you big stud, shoot that load, show us how glad you are to see us here," the guy holding my cock said mockingly.

"Bastards!!" I said angrily.

"Okay you two, get back on his big tits," the guy who had sucked my lips said commandingly to his two buddies. "I'm going to milk *another load of good stuff from this guy...*"

The two guys stood up at my sides, gloating over the look of horror in my eyes, slurped my nipples back into their mouths and the guy squatting in front of me forced me to chow down on a Viagra tablet before he gobbled my slimy cock into his mouth.

"Ohhhhh you fuckers..." I said throatily and breathlessly as my head spun and I involuntarily swallowed the tablet after the guy had wrested it into my mouth and then held my mouth closed for a few seconds so I could get it down.

God almighty, but after shooting a load my cock and man

tits are beyond sensitive...my head seemed to be really spinning... But now with a goddamned Viagra tablet flowing in me I knew I could be made to shoot my loads like crazy...GAWD!!

When I came again I screamed more in pain than pleasure, my muscular body writhing and broken out all in goose bumps.

"Oh man, oh fucking man, if I didn't see it with my own eyes I wouldn't have believed it," one of the guys said in awe. "He just shot three full loads of jizz."

"Yeah, that Viagra is the stuff that dreams are made of; and now it's our turn," one of the other guys said and stepped behind me.

"Oh shiiiit, SHIT, ohhhhh no, no," I grunted as I felt his big hands spreading my ass cheeks apart, exposing my raunchy hole. "Th-this is more than an outrage now you blasted mugs!! ARHHHHHH FUCK!!!!"

"You got it bud, fuck, that's the word here," the guy behind me said as he slowly slid his big white cock into me. "Bet your hole is feelin' real sensitive now too huh? Fuck it man, after shooting your load it's got to be REALLY sensitive back here..."

That said he wrapped his arms around me, grabbed my nipples tight, and plowed deeper and deeper into me with each damned thrust... I saw the other two guys grinning from ear to ear, waiting their turns...

My head spun and I swear I saw stars and dazzling lights in front of me as the bastard fucked my poor hole. I was in a dizzying pain and helpless to do anything about it...

They took turns fucking the tar out of my poor ass, slapping my ass cheeks hard at the same time, squeezing the bejesus out of them, and all of them reaching around me to squeeze my swollen and overly erect nipples as they fucked and fucked me...

"ARRRGHHHHHH!!!" I roared in sheer anger as one of the guys pumped my ass with his white cock. "Fucking bastards, sleazy perverts..."

"Ohhh yeah, I'm goin' to cum you guys, right in this stud's

manhole too," the guy presently fucking me chortled in my ear, slurping my earlobe, holding tight to my nipples.

I felt his warm juices flood my hole and my head spun some more...

After they had all shot their loads into my hole they squatted behind me, held my ass cheeks apart, and licked and sucked as much of their cum out of my hole as possible. I gasped breathlessly as their tongues literally invaded my most private crevice, licked at it, sucked it, and slurped on it like crazy. When they were finally done I felt like one really beat to shit black guy. The three guys got dressed and Cleeve and Otis ushered them out of the room. I stood there with my head hanging down, breathing frantically...

Later that day Cleeve and Otis brought me to another room in the house, which looked sort of, like a gym. I was coming to realize that there seemed to be an endless amount of playrooms of sorts in Cleeve and Otis' big house. It was more like an erotic house of horrors if you asked me. This room was for all intents and purposes an exercise room, but at the moment it was to be the next place where I would be used and abused, tortured and sexually accosted...

The two men tied me to a long bench press stretched out on my back, my wrists clasped together, yanked above me, and tied off to a weight bar on a rack behind the bench. Lying there on my back, my feet spread around the bench and on the floor, my upper body trussed just under my massive chest to the bench I looked up despondently. I watched as my two captors tied my big wrists tightly to the weight bar. They had better than five hundred pounds on that bar, insuring that I wouldn't be able to move it in an effort to pull myself free. As they tied me my cock was pointing straight up, long, beefy, and hard. (Can you believe that shit? First of all I didn't know why my big cock was betraying me by being so hard and excited feeling while guys were using me, GUYS, GAWD, and secondly, after all the times I had shot my load it amazed me that I was hard and erect at all. Like the man said earlier, that Viagra really is the stuff that dreams are made of.) My balls were resting on the bench between my spread legs. Then, after my wrists were securely tied to the heavier than heavy weight bar I watched helplessly as Cleeve tied a rope around and around the base of my balls, a gleeful yet sadistic expression on his face.

"Bastards, what's this shit for?" I asked them miserably. "Gyms and weight benches are meant to be used for exercise, not to tie some poor guy up in."

Without a word the two men squatted at my sides and each of them slurped one of my nipples into their mouths. The way my chest was tied to the bench made my man tits really look all jutted up and nice and appetizing let me tell you.

"Unnnnghhhhhhhh!!!" I gasped and leaned my head back. "Fuckin' tit hungry bastards…"

So there I was, totally naked, totally vulnerable, and tied to a workout bench being mauled by those two insane kidnappers. At this point I had gotten somewhat used to having my poor nipples tortured. As they worked my nipples Cleeve grabbed my hard cock in his hand and stroked it a few times… My tied balls bounced painfully back and forth between my legs, lifted up off the bench for a second or two. Unbelievably I shot my load all over the floor in front of me as Cleeve held my cock pointed straight out, stroking the fuck out of it…

"ARRRHHHHHHH, fuck," I roared and saliva foamed out of the sides of my mouth.

I lifted my head up and looked down at my captors, still working the tar out of my poor sore nipples.

"Fuckin' leave my man tits alone already you fuckers!!" I pleaded angrily.

A few minutes later they did stop working my nipples and while Otis held my head up by the back of my neck Cleeve proceeded to tie a long red silk cloth over my eyes, blindfolding me.

"H-hey… Wh-what the fuck're you blindfoldin' me for man???" I asked in terror.

"The gentleman who's coming to see you is a rather

famous and public figure," Otis responded, his hand caressing the back of my neck as he held my head up so that Cleeve could get the blindfold situated on me correctly. "He doesn't want to risk you seeing who he is when he gets here to meet and uh, eat you…"

The two men laughed hysterically. Cleeve told me that the customer who was coming had sent the red silk blindfold specially.

"Fuck man, this is scary," I said in the total darkness now.

Still laughing the two men left me alone to await the arrival of the so-called mystery man.

"Fucking kidnappers!!" I seethed angrily.

I would venture to guess that maybe a half-hour went by while I lay there tied to the workout bench, blindfolded, trapped and terrified. Then, I heard the door to the gym room open and a soft-spoken voice-saying thank you to Cleeve and Otis for this rare and special opportunity. Then the door closed. Even blind-folded I knew that someone was in the room with me.

"Who's there?" I called out. "Take this damned blindfold off and let me see who you are Fucker!!"

I smelled rich and fragrant cigar smoke and in response to my plea I felt a hand caress the top of my head, running slowly through my short-cropped hair. Whoever he was he moved his hand down the sides of my cheeks and then he cupped my chin in his hand. He held my head in a position so that he was look-ing down into my blindfolded eyes and so that I was looking up at him, but of course not seeing him. He then whispered, "This is more than a dream come true for me." At the sound of his voice my breath came in short gasps. Could it have been who I thought it was?? Was it even remotely possible? Were Cleeve and Otis that influential? No, it could not be, it just could not fucking be… but the cigar…and the accent…

"Did Cleeve and Otis tell you what I expect of you?" he asked me, running the tip of a finger over one of my very erect, very swollen, and very sore nipples.

"N-no, actually they didn't man," I replied and received a face full of cigar smoke. "Th-they don't tell me much, except to obey what the customers want. *Man, they kidnapped me Mister!!!*"

"You are going to smoke cigars," he said to me sounding impatient and then placed a lit stogy between my quivering lips. "One there in your sweet thick lipped mouth and another you'll smoke through your pussy hole."

I nearly bit down hard on the cigar he'd placed in my mouth at the sound of him calling my raunchy ass hole a pussy hole. Instead I inhaled it deeper than I had intended to. Amazingly I didn't choke, seeing as I'm not a smoker.

"Now, I want you to lift your legs as high as possible," he said to me in a somewhat commanding tone of voice. "That way I can get this other cigar inside you."

I balled my hands into fists and with no choice whatsoever in the matter I did as I was told, lifting my big feet off the bench as high as possible. It felt like I was doing stomach crunches actually.

"Will you be able to hold your feet up there or will I have to tie them above you to the weight bar along with your wrists?" he asked me, squeezing one of my feet.

I nodded "yes"; the thought of being tied in the position he'd just described unthinkable.

"Okay then, but the first time you lower your feet they get tied to the weight bar," he said and I felt the wet end of the cigar being inserted into my sweaty and mangy hole.

"Ayyyyyrrrrrr," I grunted around the cigar in my mouth and at the odd feeling invasion.

"Get those pussy lips wrapped tight around this thing," he said sternly.

I flexed my ass muscles and did as he said. He inserted the cigar further yet inside me. I puffed on the one in my mouth, feeling the ashes flicking over my neck and chest.

"When I take it out of your hole I'll smoke it with your raunchy pussy taste on it," he said to me. "Then I'm going to plow you like a field…"

I held back a gulp and felt his tongue slather over one of my sweaty feet. I heard him taking puffs on his cigar while I puffed one and another smoldered in my hole…

"I think this whole scene is very kinky," he said to me and took the cigar out of my mouth.

"Th-they're using me as a sex toy man," I said softly.

"So I was told," he said to me and I heard him puffing the cigar that had just been in my mouth. "I paid more than five hundred dollars for my time here with you Stud."

This time I did gulp, hard…

"Mmmmm, this cigar with your mouth taste on it is real sweet," he commented and trailed a finger over my blindfolded eyes. "Not to mention how sexy you look with my red silk blindfold tied over your eyes."

"Pl-please man, help me," I whispered. "Those guys kidnapped me."

"Yes I know," he said and I could feel him smiling meanly.

My legs felt awful in the position they were in. I wished like crazy that he would get the damned cigar out of my hole and do his thing already, much as I knew how much it was going to smart when he got down to fucking me. Sweating like crazy I did my best to hold my legs up as he had ordered me.

"D-do you think you overpaid for me man?" I asked him, wanting to make conversation, wanting to avoid the inevitable when he would fuck the tar out of my poor hole.

"I don't think so," he replied, gave one of my nipples a squeeze and smoked his cigar. "Looking at you the way you are right now I get the feeling I did okay financially."

Then, I felt him tug on the cigar that was jammed in my hole.

"Loosen your pussy lips now," he said with authority.

I again did as he said and heard the sound of contentment purr from him as he placed the cigar in his mouth.

"Ah yes, even better than my wife's pussy," he mused and

I grimaced as he blew smoke in my blindfolded face.

For a few minutes he sat next to me on another bench in total silence, reached over to squeeze my nipples, toyed with the knot in my blindfold, and even made me take a few puffs on the ass hole-tasting cigar. Oh fuck, I never knew that my hole could taste so bad man. Fuck, fuck, fuck, I had no choice but to do whatever the hell he wanted... Alas, he didn't give me permission to lower my legs and by then they were in immense pain. "AYYYYYYRRRR," I found myself ranting in pain a little while later as the guy mounted me and began thrusting his hardness deep into my poor hole.

"Ah yes, oh yes, as I said, better than my wife's pussy," the cigar guy panted.

As he fucked me like a madman, my legs in the air, my feet resting on his shoulders the smell of expensive cigars filled the air.

"Ohhhhh God man, y-you've got a big meat pole," I squawked miserably.

He kissed my blindfolded eyes his cock buried deep inside me.

"Oh yes, this is worth every penny of what I spent on you, you gorgeous stud," the guy gasped, thrusting in and out of me like his life depended on it. "Even down to the red silk blindfold."

He took my ankles in hand, held them aloft and plowed into me and plowed into me and plowed into me...

Whoever the fuck he was, when he was done fucking the tar out of me, having filled my hole with his creamy mess he forced me to shoot two more loads myself. All before going to work on my nipples, running his hands slowly over my muscular chest, squeezing my big rock hard pecs. When he was done with me I was utterly exhausted. It had been a long day. I had been used to the point of feeling faint. When Cleeve and Otis untied me from the workout bench I didn't even try to struggle when they hoisted me off the floor. Instead I enjoyed the ride as they carried me out of the room and to the room where I was kept to sleep. In between having men come to use me Cleeve and Otis kept me well fed and well watered. As I said earlier, they never starved me...

On Monday while two guys were taking turns fucking my poor ass hole while I was hooked up in the wooden structure I wondered if my boss at work was wondering where I was. I am not the type to just suddenly take a day off and I'm hardly ever out sick from work. When the two guys were done fucking me they left and Cleeve and Otis took a few turns at my ass...

On Thursday morning my two captors loaded me into the back of their van. I was dressed in the suit I had been wearing on the night they had abducted me out of the park house. It was ten AM when they pushed me out the back doors of the van and into the park where they had grabbed me, tossing me out of that van like yesterday's garbage to be thrown away. I stood there with my heart pounding as the van pulled away, realizing too late that I'd failed to get the license plate number. After the van was gone I had to wonder if it had all been real, if I had truly been kid-napped. As I tried to tell myself that it had all been a bad dream, a nightmare, the pain in my hole, the soreness of my nipples and my over sensitized cock all reminded me that it had been real. It had indeed happened...

I slowly made my way home. As I walked slowly I could feel splooge dripping from my wounded asshole and staining my damned under shorts. When I finally reached home I called my boss and explained to him that I'd had a family emergency to take care of and that I would return to work the following Monday. There were several messages on the answering machine from Linda. At first she said things like she was worried about me. Then she said she had waited for me to come out of that park house for over an hour, not understanding how it could take a guy so long to pull his pants up. In another message she stated how it wasn't right that I seemed to be ignoring her phone calls. A call that I dreaded where she said that I probably thought she was a cheap woman, being that she'd wanted to make love in a public place. After listening to a few calls from Linda, my parents who were worried about me and a couple of my buddies I hit the "stop" button on the answering machine. More than anything at that moment I needed a shower, a good, long, and hot shower to be exact. After the shower I would call Linda and try to explain what had happened to me. But holy shit was I really going to tell her that I had been kidnapped and used as a sex toy? And used as a sex toy by more men than I could remember at that point? After Linda I would call my parents and then my buddies who had left messages as well. I stripped slowly out of my clothes down to my black sheer socks and stood in front of the full-length mirror in my bathroom. My poor nipples were swollen and erect…no real damage done though, my cock was sort of sore and as I said overly sensitized from constantly being sucked, but so help me I was still able to get it up with no goddamned problem.

"Tyrone, you are still the man," I murmured with a grin.

Then, I took my big cock in hand, thought of Cleeve and Otis, and slowly stroked myself… I also thought of Linda and wondered if I could get her to appreciate my big feet a little more…

The End

About the Author

Christopher Trevor was born in July 1963 and grew up in New York City. As soon as he was old enough to know how he began writing fiction and has been writing gay erotic/fetish stories for the past ten to twelve years at this point. He became an avid reader as well from the time he knew how and reads everything from fiction, to non-fiction to biographies of interesting and unusual people, people who have made a difference or who have paved the way for others. Christopher attributes his writing artistic inspiration to artists such as Etienne, Tom of Finland, Tagame, The Hun, and most notably Joe T, who Christopher has had the pleasure of speaking with and even meeting over the last few years. Christopher states, "Joe T encouraged me to write about my fetish because I was embarrassed about it at the time. Joe T said that when we are embarrassed about something that makes it even more enticing somehow." Christopher totally agreed and never stopped writing in this genre. Erotic writers who inspired Christopher Trevor were: Tom Shaw (author of "That Day at the Quarry), C.S. White (author of Big Sur), Larry Townsend (author of countless erotic novels), and Mason Powell (author of the classic story "The Brig.")

Christopher discovered that not only did he enjoy writing erotic tales but that after his first bondage experience he had a genuine flair for it. Writing to erotic oriented magazines about his first bondage experience truly opened the floodgates for Christopher where this style of writing is concerned. Christopher thanks the handsome and muscular "Greg" for that experience way back in time. Christopher took "Creative Writing" courses every semester during his high school years and while other friends of his stopped writing what they loved to write about as time went on Christopher never let a day go by when he didn't write something… "I feel that if I don't write every day I will die," Christopher has said many times over.

Foot fetish stories and all things related; spanking fetish, erotic shaving, muscle bondage, tickle torture, and hardcore stories are just a few of the areas of gay eroticism that Christopher enjoys writing about and inspiring in others as well. As one internet buddy said to Christopher where the black socks fetish is concerned, "Until I started talking with you I never gave a thought to my socks when I got dressed for work in the morning. Now when I pull my dress socks on every morning I get a chill up my spine."

Christopher is proud of the erotic effect he has on people…

Christopher Trevor is also the author of:

The Executive Guide to Foot Fetishism and Office Discipline
1-887895-36-1

Executive Ties That Bind
1-887895-37-X

Don't!! Stop!! That Tickles!!
1-887895-31-0

The Taming of Dominick
1-887895-45-0

Timmy and The Hong Kong Tailor
1-887895-30-2

Love, Torture and Redemption
1-887895-32-9

Timmys Ticklish Trials
978-1-887895-74-3

The Gym Instructor
978-1-887895-44-6

Milked
978-1-887895-66-8

Look for them where you found this book or Goodboner.com.

www.ingramcontent.com/pod-product-compliance
Lightning Source LLC
Chambersburg PA
CBHW071225260626
47162CB00004B/1423